A Gamer's Wish

Book 1 of the Hidden Wishes Series
A GameLit Novel

by

Tao Wong

Copyright

This is a work of fiction. Names, characters, businesses, places, events, and incidents are either the products of the author's imagination or used in a fictitious manner. Any resemblance to actual persons, living or dead, or actual events is purely coincidental.

No part of this publication may be reproduced, distributed, or transmitted in any form or by any means, including photocopying, recording, or other electronic or mechanical methods, without the prior written permission of the publisher, except in the case of brief quotations embodied in critical reviews and certain other non-commercial uses permitted by copyright law.

No part of this book may be used or reproduced in any manner for the purpose of training artificial intelligence technologies or systems.

Books in the Hidden Universe

Hidden Wishes

A Gamer's Wish

A Squire's Wish

A Jinn's Wish

Hidden Dishes

The Nameless Restaurant

Chaotic Aperitifs

Thaumaturgic Tapas

Sorcerous Plates

Table of Contents

Chapter 1

Simple curiosity. That was all it took to change my world.

My life changed with a black briefcase one spring evening. It had a 1960s design, a perfect rectangle made of black leather with a number-combination lock, still in pristine condition. It was the fifth and last piece of luggage I had purchased earlier that day at the lost luggage auction—and the most expensive piece. Unless I was really lucky, I might make enough for a week's groceries from all this. At some point, I knew that I had to find a new job, but lucky for me, retail jobs were a dime a dozen right now. If you were willing to take late-night shifts at least. Still, that was a concern for future me.

Luggage like this always left me wondering about its story. The smell of the leather, the faintest hint as I held it to my nose, told me it was probably genuine. Maybe it was a hipster throwback, a handmade piece for people with more money than sense, but something told me it was the real deal. A genuine 1960s briefcase. That raised a number of questions: Was it an old purchase, set aside and never used till recently? Perhaps given to a new graduate, a present to commemorate their graduation? Did someone buy it at a thrift store, a discarded piece of luggage that wasn't wanted or needed till it was unceremoniously lost and abandoned again? That was, after all, how it had come into my possession. The airport auctioned off uncollected lost luggage every sixty days after it entered the system.

I sat silently for a time as I ran my hands along the briefcase and made up stories about its former owner, the briefcase, and what I might find within. Small stories, daydreams of the kinds of things I'd find inside—a laptop, a journal, maybe a calculator for an accountant. Business cards, of course. It was a briefcase. I took my time because this was half the fun of buying lost luggage—the stories I got to make up before the inevitable disappointment of reality. And while I thought, I ran my fingers along the numerical lock and attempted to open the case.

Click.

Four-six-seven. I idly noted the number that worked before I continued my attempts on the opposite side. It took another two minutes, an impatient two minutes as I found myself suddenly anxious to see what I had bought. When the click came, I held my breath for a second before I finally opened the briefcase to see my prize.

A leather journal, a single, expensive-looking fountain pen, and a capped bottle of ink snuggly fit into an inkwell dominated one side of the briefcase. On the other side, a series of nine small boxes with carved runes on top of them sat in what had to be a custom-made enclosure. I frowned as I traced the runes, never having seen anything like them before. Not that I was any expert, mind you, but they sure were pretty. On the underside of the top of the briefcase was a simple, silver-lined mirror that reflected my image to me.

Wavy brown hair that was about two weeks overdue for a haircut, slanted brown eyes that I had been told were my best feature and thin lips reflected back at me. I rubbed my chin, realizing I had forgotten to shave again and grown a sparse, stubbly goatee. It was a bad habit, but shaving was never a priority when you only had to do it every few weeks. Just another gift of being ethnically southern Chinese. At twenty-eight, I was glad I'd finally gotten out of the "baby face" period of my life, even if I was still occasionally mocked for looking like I was in my early twenties. That was okay, considering some of those same mockers were already losing their hair.

Initial perusal over, I began the process of stripping the briefcase. I started with the book first and found, to my surprise, it was empty. Nothing was on the front page or any of the succeeding pages. It had very nice binding though and high-quality leather. I'd probably make a few dollars selling it online. The fountain pen was an old dip-and-write type, might have been worth something to a collector. I capped the pen and put it away carefully. The ink I pulled out and set aside with the rest of the junk. No money in reselling used ink.

Lastly, I started opening the boxes. And that's when things started getting weird. The first box held scales; the second, a series of dead beetles; the third, feathers from a single type of bird; and the fourth, old, dark earth. After the second box, I grabbed the garbage and started tossing contents into it immediately. Perhaps this had been owned by a taxidermist? Or a naturalist?

"Oww!" I howled and shook my hand. When I had touched the fifth box, what must have been the accumulated static charge of living in a basement apartment had shocked me. It had never been that bad before, but I made a mental note to get a humidifier… when I had the money.

Gingerly, I touched the box and, finding the charge gone, I opened it, ready to toss its contents away. Instead, I found a simple signet ring made of a dark metal. Or alloy of metals. I frowned as I plucked the ring out and rubbed at it to clean it up, curious to see what it was made of.

As I said, curiosity changed my life.

***

"Are you done yet?" the blond woman, who had formed in my apartment from smoke, asked me. Clad in a pink bra, tiny vest, and billowy sheer pants, she reminded me of an actress from an old, cheesy TV show, almost uncannily so. Seriously, the blond genie that stood in front of me with her sardonic smile would have sent copyright lawyers salivating at the fees they'd earn. If they could have seen her. And if she hadn't wished them away.

"You… you're a genie! But that was a ring, not a lamp!" I spluttered, the ring that the smoke had streamed from still clutched in my hand in a death grip.

"Jinn! And yes, I am. What may I do for you, Master?" the genie said. Turning her head, she looked around my bachelor suite with a flicker of distaste. "Maybe a bigger residence?"

"You're a genie…" I stared at the blonde, my mind caught in a circular trap as it struggled with the insanity in front of it. After all, genies didn't exist. But there, in front of me, was a genie.

"Oh, hell. I really can't wait for this entire 'enlightenment' period to be over," the genie said with a roll of her eyes after I just continued to stare at her blankly. She turned away from me and walked around the room before she stopped at my micro-kitchen to open the fridge. Bent over, she fished inside before extracting day-old fried rice and popping a bite into her mouth. A conjured spoon later, she was digging into last night's dinner and prodding my stove, flat-screen TV, and laptop. "What is this?"

"Fried rice."

"I know what fried rice is. And this isn't bad," she complimented me, ignoring my mumbled thanks while she pointed at the TV screen and then laptop. "This. And this."

"TV and laptop."

"Huh." She returned to the TV before she prodded at it a few more times and inevitably adjusted its angle. "That's amazing. I guess your science actually does have some use. Well, outside of indoor plumbing. That isn't as good."

My brain finally stopped going in circles after I decided to stop trying to actually understand what was going on. If I had a genie in my house, I had a genie. "So, your name isn't Jeannie, is it?"

"Do I look like a Jeannie to you?"

"Well…"

"The Seven Seals!" The genie flickered, and the previously blonde creature transformed into a black-haired, hawk-nosed Middle-Eastern woman…with considerably less clothing than before, which should have been a challenge. "Call me Lily. What's yours?"

"Uhh…"

"Aaargh!" Lily stared at her clothing and then stared at me for a moment. A second later, she was clad in a T-shirt that said "I Aim to Misbehave" and a pair of jeans. I would admit I found the new clothing options even more distracting, especially since they were an exact replica of what I was wearing.

"I'm Henry. And what was that about?"

"Nothing. Nothing at all," Lily snapped at me and waved her spoon at my laptop. "What is a 'laptop'?"

"A portable computer," I explained.

"No, I've seen a computer before. They take up rooms three times the size of your… residence," Lily said, prodding my laptop.

"Computers haven't been that big since the fifties. Okay, maybe sixties. And I guess there are supercomputers that are that big these days," I blathered on. "But most people don't really need a supercomputer. I mean, all I do with mine is play some games and get on the Internet."

"Internet?" Lily raised her spoon. "Wait. Stop. Two things: what year is this, and do you have more food?"

"Twenty eighteen, and there's some pizza in the freezer," I said. "What year did you think this was?"

"That explains why the enchantments have faded," Lily said as she finished raiding my fridge. She stared at the pizza and then looked at me imploringly. I sighed and helped her add it to the microwave, which I then had to explain to her. That certainly dated her further, putting her at least into the 1960s, which was around the same time as the briefcase. Once the pizza was ready and the genie was eating, I got back to the important questions.

"What enchantments?"

"All of them, of course. They really should have closed off the runes between the concealment and defensive enchantments. If they'd asked me, I could have told them. But of course, they never do," Lily said, shaking her head. "Once the enchantment wasn't being regularly recharged, the concealment rune started draining the rest. Took it about fifty years or so, at a guess. Good thing for you they were sloppy; otherwise, you'd be dead."

"Dead?"

"Oh, yes. Heart attack when you failed the third time on opening the briefcase," Lily said. "Always a good defensive spell—few creatures can survive without a heart. Well, except the undead, but they wouldn't be able to even touch the briefcase with the wards against them."

"I could have died," I said weakly as I stumbled to my bed and sat down with a thud.

"Blazing suns." Lily sat down across from me. "You humans are always so damn sensitive about your mortality."

I sat there in silence and stared at the far wall, my brain refusing to work any further at this new revelation. Genies. Magic. My death. There is a certain point in an individual's day when one just can't go on, and I'd hit that point. Without speaking, I flopped onto my bed, grabbed my comforter, and rolled into a ball.

***

When I woke hours later, the sun had set, and my basement apartment was shrouded in darkness. I exhaled in relief, grateful but slightly disappointed that the blond/brunette genie had been but a weird dream. Paper rustled, and I twisted my head to the side to spot a pair of glowing red eyes bent over a book.

"Well, that was a very manly scream," Lily said, hiding a smirk.

"You… what are you doing?" I gulped, clutching my comforter to my body after I finally managed to turn on my bedside light. The additional illumination drove the fire from her eyes, making them look human again. I recalled the flames that lit her face from within, doubting I'd ever forget them. Not demonic though… at least, they didn't feel demonic. Just otherworldly.

"Hmmm? Reading. You have quite a selection here." Lily nodded to the bookcases that lined the walls of my apartment. I will admit books are one of my indulgences. The books are wide ranging, covering everything from history to fiction. Really, I just grabbed whatever seemed interesting when I hit a garage sale.

"It wasn't a dream," I muttered to myself and put my head between my knees.

"Yes, yes. Are you going to have a breakdown again, or are we finally getting to the part where you make a wish?" Lily said, bored. "If you want to wait, I've still got two books in this series to finish."

"Don't bother. The author's still not done book six after six years. So magic really is real?" I said, my voice muffled by the comforter. "And you're a genie. Like, 'rub the lamp and get three wishes' kind of genie."

"Yes, and I'm a jinn, not a genie, and sort of," Lily said absently as she continued to read.

"Sort of?" I latched on to the wishy-washy word.

"I'm not actually bound to fulfill all three wishes since what I can do is limited by the ring and my powers," Lily said and then, when I said nothing, looked up and explained further. "If you wished for the sun to go out, I wouldn't be able to do it, and you'd have wasted my power in trying. And annoyed like a hundred gods at the same time. I am also bound to the ring, not a lamp, unlike what Antoinne might have written."

"Antoinne?" I shook my head. No. I was not going to get distracted. It was hard enough keeping my head on straight. "Magic is real." I could not keep the wonder from my voice as I said that. In a world of mediocrity and the mundane, magic was real.

"Always has been."

"But how did I not know of it?"

"Your world of science and rational thought blinded you to the arcane. What cannot be explained was relegated to hidden corners of the world, and rare as the gift is, it is no wonder humanity forgot. Magic is still practiced in back alleys and small towns. The supernatural world still exists, but it is more than happy to be forgotten. After all, humanity has never been kind to what it considers others."

"You've given that speech before," I said, and Lily nodded. "All right then, so magic is real, and you're a ge—" At her pointed stare, I corrected myself. "Jinn, and I have three wishes. Is there anything I shouldn't wish for?"

"Life. Death. The fate of countries. Time travel. I can alter the minds and physical reactions of others but not their souls; I cannot make someone love you or stop hating you, just lust for you or perhaps temper their physical reactions to your presence," Lily answered promptly. As I nodded along, she opened her mouth and then shut it.

"You were going to say something."

"I was."

"What was it?"

"It doesn't matter."

"Why not?" I leaned forward in my chair. I wished the light shone better on her face. At least then I would have a better view of it. There was something in her voice.

Lily stayed silent for a time, obviously fighting something internally. In the end, her lips twisted wryly, and she waved a hand in front of my bookcases, causing them to glow slightly. "Because you won't listen."

"That's a bit insulting. You don't know me," I said, and she laughed, her laughter brittle and high.

"I know you. I've known a hundred thousand like you. My masters never listen," Lily said with a smile. "So tell me your wish."

I almost snapped back that I wished she would tell me what she was going to say. Almost. But annoyed or not, I was not going to waste my chance at real magic, at a real chance to change my world. "You don't know me, and I don't know you. So why don't you tell me, and maybe, maybe we'll come to know one another."

Lily stared at me for a long time, her eyes glowing red before she finally spoke, her voice weary. "I am bound by the ring to fulfill your wishes, but I am not omniscient. I can only change what I understand, and I am not responsible for the consequences of any changes. Not that it'll stop you from blaming me."

I stared at Lily for a time, then slowly nodded. "You're saying if I made a wish, you'd be forced to make it happen even if it was a silly wish. Like, if I wished for a million dollars right this second, you'd be forced to make it appear right in this room. Maybe as bills, maybe as dollar coins, which probably would suck."

"I am not malicious, no matter what you people might say," Lily said. "But most wishes for wealth are not well thought out. I once gave a goatherder a mountain of gold, and he and his family were killed for it. A hundred years ago, a gentleman asked for a million pounds. Of course, I had never seen the kind of notes they used, so I made the bank notes for him, a million dollars' worth, all exactly the same. He was unhappy about that."

I slowly nodded, staring at her. "You're not all-powerful and all-knowing, just powerful. Like a giant hammer wielded by toddlers."

"Yes!" Lily said, excited for a second.

I grunted, closing my eyes. The worse part was that I was the damn toddler. But still… magic was real.

I had not realized I had spoken that thought aloud till that whisper echoed through the basement. Into the silence, she slowly spoke. "Do you desire magic then?"

"With every fiber of my being," I answered honestly. "But I can see a million, billion ways it could go wrong. Wish for magic, and I might get the ability without the knowledge to wield it. Wish for knowledge and ability, and you'd stick it all in my head and maybe make me go crazy while doing it. Wish for a mentor, and, well, it might be a black mage who comes in."

"You did listen." Lily's lips twisted into a wry smile. "Though, again, not directly malicious. If you wished for the knowledge to wield magic, and that alone, I'd probably only insert enough that you would not be driven mad."

"You can do that?" I blinked, having rattled off my words without thought. I hadn't actually expected her to know how to inject information into my head.

"Of course. I'm a jinn who has been in the service of some of the greatest mages this world has ever known. I am no dotard myself," Lily boasted. "Adding knowledge direct would be no different than creating a magical book of learning. In fact, it would be simpler without the preservation and containment spells."

"Huh," I said, rubbing my chin and staring at the girl. "So, it's not the amount of knowledge but the speed."

"Close enough," she said, and I grunted.

"I guess I'd have to level up first."

"Level up?" Lily asked, and I waved my hand toward my bookshelf where my RPG books were neatly stacked from D&D's first editions to more recent RPGs, indie and mainstream publishers. "One second." She muttered that word and then shimmered for a brief moment, a second at most, and suddenly all the books were stacked neatly around her. "How interesting. Entire universes written and governed by rules and dice."

"Did you just read all of them with super speed?" I asked.

"Not super speed. That's always more trouble than its worth. You have to deal with friction and air resistance and heat. I prefer to slow time," Lily said nonchalantly. "I do see what you mean. These 'levels' characters have limit their growth, giving them knowledge and strength as they pass each milestone."

"You're saying it's possible? For me to wield magic if we put it in a game system?" I said excitedly, fallen hopes rising again like a rocket at her words.

"Of course. Who do you think you're talking to?" Lily asked.

"Perfect!" I paused, frowning as I worked out the implications. Perhaps I had found a way to cheat the system. "All right. One last question - how do I know everything you've said is true?"

At those words, even in the dim light, I saw Lily's face twist with quickly concealed hurt. She looked away for a second and then back at me. "Well, that's the rub, isn't it? You can't."

That was the rub. It wasn't as if I could look this up on Snopes or jump on Quora, seeking expert advice. The stories I did know of, they conflicted. The original stories of jinn said they were like us, neither good nor evil, creatures of free will like humanity itself. Since then, they'd been both friend and foe in a myriad of stories. Of course, it wasn't as if I knew how to tell which were true or fake.

In the end, it came down to trust. Could I, should I, trust Lily? Did it matter though? By her own admission, anything I wished for needed her interpretation. Of course that too could have been a lie. But for a chance at magic, however slim it might be, I would take it.

With that thought, I smiled and leaned forward. "All right, so here's what I was thinking."

Chapter 2

-Hours later and—at Lily's insistence—a bunch of Thai takeout later, we'd gone back and forth on the game system we might implement. Crouched over pad thai, red curry, and pineapple fried rice, I argued with a raven-haired jinn about the merits of game systems.

"We should skip character creation entirely," Lily said, waving a pair of chopsticks at me with an egg roll still held in them. "You don't want to go through the most equitable way of doing so—"

"I'm not letting you roll for my attributes. I am not going to risk getting a three on intelligence," I interrupted.

Lily continued without pausing at my interruption. "We should just avoid it altogether. Unintended consequences, remember?"

"But a base ten stat option and a number of points with the ability to increase and decrease the attributes would give me more ability to customize myself," I argued back.

"Yes, yes. Not only do we risk angering the gods if we do it that way, there's the actual work involved. I still have to physically alter you to make it happen. If you doubled your existing strength, I'd have to balance various muscles, tendons, and ligaments to make sure you don't tear yourself apart the moment you move. And strength's the easiest. I mean, constitution? What is that? Your immune system?" Lily asked. "And don't even get me started on wisdom."

"You've said. And of course, willpower is the soul, which you can't touch," I muttered. "So I guess no altering attributes when I level up either? Fine. We'll skip character creation and direct changes to my body, just pure knowledge."

"Well, one change - I've got to open your magical pathways," Lily corrected, a finger held up.

"Ah. Right…" I frowned, eyebrows drawn together as I stared at her. "How complicated is that?"

Lily held her hand up horizontal and waggled it sideways, then snagged the last piece of chicken from the curry. Seeing my flat stare, she said, "It depends on how innately gifted you are. The more gifted, the harder it's going to be."

"Isn't it the other way around?" I frowned, and she shook her head.

"No. Because if you're already gifted, you should be using magic already. If you aren't, you've simply got a blockage that I'll need to remove," Lily explained.

"That's going to hurt, isn't it?"

"Yup!" Lily said, way too cheerfully, as she poured curry on her rice. "We should order more."

"What is it with you and food? Can't you just conjure it?" I asked.

"Conjured food never tastes right. There's always something missing. Now, I saw a menu for Greek?"

For an all-powerful jinn who was about to change my world, she certainly seemed to be costing me more than she earned. As I walked toward the fridge to grab the takeout menu, I pulled out my wallet and stared at the last few dollars I had. Well, it would be worth it.

"This is a computer game?" Lily asked, poking at my screen.

I smacked her finger away, growling. "Stop that. You're going to leave prints."

"One, owww!" Lily waved her hand. "Two, I don't leave prints. This body isn't exactly corporeal like yours."

"Still. Don't touch the screen. And yes, this is a computer version of the games we've been talking about. This is a single-player game where you control a party. It's a bit dated these days, but it's quite fun," I explained. "This is my saved game, which lets me start from where I left off. Character creation is done, and this is my inventory…"

***

"No skills?"

"Too complicated. I'd have to either give you all or nothing. What would we use as a basis? All these systems are too broad; unless you want to end up forgetting how to swim simply because your athletics are zero. I mean, who designs these things? Swimming, gymnastics, hurdling, and sprinting all under the same skill?" Lily clicked around my computer screen.

"Can't you just give me a low rating for a bunch of skills I should know?"

"No. You can't handle it." Lily waved her hands, fluttering her fingers apart. "A point in, say, science might do that. Or we could get granular and then realize we forgot some important skill like typing. You wouldn't be able to use this computer of yours because you'll automatically fail every attempt."

"Ugh… okay."

***

"Perks?"

"My ring might consider that cheating." Lily rubbed her chin. "I could do weaknesses."

"Hard no."

Lily giggled at my reaction, flipping to the next page in the book while she stabbed a portion of tiramisu. "Equipment's out, same as perks."

"Well, shit." I rubbed my temples, staring into space. "Way I see this, all I'm getting is the ability to use magic at a gradated level."

"All?"

"Fine, fine. It's a lot," I said, waving my hands at her. I knew it was a lot. It was more than I'd had a day ago. And yet, I felt cheated. My eyes burned, and my heart ached, exhaustion finally kicking my doors down.

"Damn right it's a lot. If we do this right, you might be the first archmagi I've ever been able to create with my wishes," Lily said. "You need to rest."

"Yeah… yeah." I glanced at the single bed in the apartment. "Do you… I mean, well…"

"I'll rest in my ring if I need to," Lily said, waving me to bed.

I nodded numbly, lying back down. As I drifted off to sleep, I wondered if leaving an unbound magical being—that some might consider evil—to run around unchecked and alone was a good idea. As I rolled onto my side, I stared blearily at the raven-haired jinn who was idly chewing on a strand of hair, brows furrowed in concentration as she clicked away on her mouse, killing cows and picking up loot.

***

Light streamed in from the single basement window when I slowly woke up. The continuous *click, click, click* of a mouse, the occasional stab of a keyboard key, and a repetitive fantasy soundtrack punctuated the silence, making me think I was back in my college dorm with Wynn. That man had been obsessed with his 4X games. I rolled over to tell him to lower the damn volume, and I spotted discarded food containers, a pair of unwashed glasses with the last of my orange juice in them, and a stack of books. However, instead of an overweight gamer with bad hygiene, I saw a toned and very feminine body hunched over my laptop with a face that could have graced a celebrity magazine.

"Have you been up all night?" I muttered as I swung my feet over the edge of the bed. Daylight hit my eyes, and I automatically twitched my head to the side—hiding in the shadows—and corrected myself. "Day."

"Yes. I'm level forty-seven now. Just took the portal back to town. My inventory's full—"

"You know, you were supposed to be doing research."

"This is research. And you need a bath," Lily said, sniffing.

"Me? You—" Well, if she didn't leave fingerprints, who said she sweated or had any of the other grody side effects of having a physical body? Surreptitiously, I sniffed myself and wrinkled my nose. Well, she had a point.

A quick shower later, I was standing over my coffee pot as I contemplated the remnants of my kitchen. What should have lasted me a week had been consumed overnight, leaving me with two slices of bread and the jam to go with it. As I made my meager breakfast, I said, "Did you learn anything?"

"A lot. I like these computer games better than your tabletop ones. No skills, character creation is simplified, no need to create backstory or hooks for your GM… experience is received from quests that are clearly defined, and development of abilities is clear," Lily said, never looking up. "I think we can work with this. I can even give you all these bars, but they'd be estimations. So, something like health wouldn't be reality. You could still die from smacking your head too hard."

"Really? Do you think we're ready?" I sat next to her and placed my sandwich on the table beside me. Without even looking away from the computer, she snagged half of my sandwich.

"Sure. Sure… hey, how do you pass into the level forty-seven boss chamber?"

"Ah…" I squinted, staring at the game and racking my brain. "Eh… check the Internet for a guide."

"Guide," Lily said, slowly and carefully.

I reached over and paused her game, then tabbed over to a browser. In a few seconds, I had a guide open. Before I could even scroll down, the laptop was snatched back, and Lily perused the level.

"Ooh… I missed this portion entirely."

I coughed into my hand, dragging her attention back to me. "My wish?"

"Sure, sure. No character creation, no skills, magic and knowledge that's gradated by levels, and level-appropriate quests so you don't die fighting a dragon on your first day," Lily said distractedly as she chewed on her hair. "I wonder what I missed earlier…"

Oh, hell. She was a completist. I rubbed my eyes. "And the ability to add patches if we realize we missed something."

"Patches. Right. Right. Sure. That your wish?"

"Yes, I just—"

"Great!" Her hand raised and waved at me before I could finish my sentence… and then pain.

My nerves felt like molten fire had been poured along them, my entire body gone rigid as muscles locked. I tasted blood after I accidentally bit my tongue, its copper taste and blueberry jam mixing in my mouth. A moment later, an ice pick slammed into my brain, and the world shimmered and distorted in my vision. Light shifted and broke apart, and through my screams, I heard a bell chiming before a new wave of pain hit me. My existence became the pain, the twisting in my bones and nerves before I finally fell and passed out.

***

When I woke up, I found the raven-haired jinn leaning over me. She was dabbing at my face with a wet cloth that was speckled with blood. My head felt like someone had decided to use it as a punching bag, but at least the pain in my body had fallen away to a dull but constant thrum, reminiscent of a deep muscular ache. As my eyes opened, Lily offered me a pair of pills, which I gratefully took and washed down with the cup of water she proffered.

It was only after I had swallowed them that I thought to check. "What was that?"

"Pain killers. It says take one, but I figured you'd need two," Lily said, offering me a chance to look at the bottle of naproxen. I sighed in relief, grateful for clear pharmaceutical labeling. After all, I did not want her to be grabbing my Imodium instead. "How are you doing?"

"Hurts," I said, being careful to move ever so slowly as I peered at her. "What was all that about?"

"I made your wish come true," Lily said, looking ever-so-slightly guilty.

"But I—" I felt a rush of anger push aside part of my pain. "I wasn't ready…"

"Yeah, sorry about that," Lily said.

"Sorry?! You could have killed me. And we haven't even discussed experience and leveling and quests and—"

"I know. I know!" Lily shouted, the loud noise making me wince. She stood up and threw her hands up toward the sky. She blushed with guilt before she calmed and squatted beside me. "I'm sorry. I… got distracted."

"Distracted? You got obsessed," I growled, and she nodded. I slumped backward with my eyes closed and forced myself to draw another deep breath. "Tell me about what you did."

"What we said we were going to do. I opened your arcane pathways and inserted the basics of magic into your mind. I have my own spells that will record your progress, and when you're ready,

I'll level you up, and you'll get your next dose of knowledge."

"About that."

"What?"

"Leveling up. How do I get experience?" I frowned as I slowly sat up. "I mean, I don't want to go out killing things if I don't have to, and—"

"Leveling is just an abstraction of your growth and development as a mage. You gain experience by practicing your magic or studying. Though…" At my pointed stare, Lily continued. "High-stress situations are extremely strong methods of acquiring knowledge. It's not just about sitting in your tower all day, reading books. The way we've set it up, you'd likely learn more this way too."

I grunted. "So, questing."

"Definitely," Lily said. "Don't worry though. I'll make sure they're level appropriate."

"There's a lot of you in this conversation," I said suspiciously, and Lily flashed me an innocent smile, even going so far as to flutter her eyelashes at me. "Lily…"

"Well, someone has to be your class trainer and GM," Lily said.

I stared at the raven-haired beauty for a time as a thought worked its way through my throbbing head. "What normally happens when a wish is granted? Or all three wishes?"

"Well… ummm…" Lily looked aside and then sighed. "Fine. I normally get banished into the ring whenever I'm not needed."

"But being my GM, you're always going to be needed," I said, completing the thought that had wormed its way in. "So even if I make my other two wishes, you'll still be free."

"Not free. Just out of the ring," Lily said seriously, pointing to the ring I had slipped onto the middle finger of my left hand. "I'm still bound to not use my powers in any meaningful way."

I mulled the thought over for some time, Lily's admission and the way she'd managed to get something out of this. I would have felt betrayed, but if I'd been trapped in a ring for fifty years, maybe I would have been as manipulative. In the end, it came down to trust… and the fact that she only stayed out for as long as I was alive.

"Henry?" Lily said, and I looked up to see her sitting nervously, waiting for me to speak. I frowned at that, at why an indescribably ancient being with the power to change reality was nervous. What could she have experienced in that time to create that level of fear?

"It's fine," I said finally. In either case, I had better things to focus on. "I can do magic now, right? How?"

"Just think about it," Lily said unhelpfully.

Instead of chiding her, I fell silent and focused. At first, my thoughts were distracted and jumbled as I thought about thinking about magic, but eventually, they settled down. It was at that point I realized I didn't need to think about it as an abstract concept; it was more like moving a muscle

I hadn't used in a while. All I had to do was want to use it.

"Light!" I muttered to myself and found my hand shifting, making the arcane signs needed.

Light Ball Cast
42% Synchronicity

The ball of light that flowed out of my palm was weak and cast a pale, fitful yellow light not even as strong as a sixty-watt bulb. On the other hand, it was mine.

"What was that?" I stared at where the words had been in the corner of my vision, gone now.

"The user interface I built in. It'll give you information about your magic and how you're doing," Lily said, smirking.

"And synchronicity?" Even as I asked, the answer was popping into mind.

Still, Lily felt the need to answer me. "As you know, magic can be cast in many ways, just like a painting can be painted with different colors. The one you've learned is older, more direct. At its earliest stages, it requires a mental and physical component—"

"The closer I synchronize both mental and physical actions, the more powerful the spell," I said, finishing for her. "And at later stages, I won't even need the physical actions."

"Correct." Lily smiled at me even as I began to add to the single floating ball. Each time a new ball was conjured, the same message would appear, telling me of my progress. After my initial cast, most sat around the 60 percent region, bouncing higher and lower as I practiced.

When nearly two dozen light balls had appeared, the first one finally flickered and died. As I reached toward the sky to cast the spell again, a blue bar appeared in the top of my vision, already mostly empty. "Is that my mana bar?"

"Close enough," Lily said before she put a hand on my arm. It was the first time we had actually touched, and I found her flesh smooth and surprisingly warm. Warm like a roll of bread freshly drawn from the oven, a comforting heat that traveled down my arm. "You should stop now. Mana, the arcane energy you wield, should never be fully depleted. The arcane powers you, your life force, and soul. Always make sure to leave a little behind."

Even as she finished, I realized my headache and the fire in my nerves had returned. In my excitement and focus, I had not noticed the growing pain. As I sat back onto the bed, Lily walked away and returned with some water for me to drink. I considered the implication of what she said and marveled at my first spell. As my head throbbed, I made a few attempts to bring my character sheet up. Status. Status screen. Character. In the end, I realized that like my magic, I just needed to actually want it with focus.

Class: Mage
Level 1 (4% Experience)
Known Spells: Light Ball, Force Bolt, Warmth, Chill, Chime, Breeze

It was strange, having the system and the knowledge in my mind. On one hand, these spells were hard-coded, distinct artifacts I could conjure with a thought. On the other hand, the knowledge imparted to me actually explained how they were all manifestations of a few alterations of the same formula. Light, Warmth, Chill, Chime, and Breeze were all about the alteration of energy, a conjuring and displacement of physical energy. It was like a punch—you could throw a jab, hook, uppercut, haymaker, and more, but in the end, they were mostly the same muscles used in different ways, broken up into distinct ideas for ease of use.

In time, with more building blocks, I could probably even make my own spells. However, I needed a lot more blocks before I could even think about that. The only real disparity in my spells was Force Bolt, my only offensive spell and also my most advanced. Even thinking about the various parts that made up the spell made my head hurt—figuratively. At a guess, I'd need more practice before I understood it. On the other hand, my rental was not the place to throw around destructive magic.

In time, the silence brought on by my thoughts—punctuated only by the clicking of the laptop after Lily returned to the computer—was broken by my stomach rumbling.

"I wasn't going to say anything, but your kitchen's empty," Lily said from behind the computer screen. "We should order more takeout."

"Har. Not happening." I shook my head and stood, the pain having receded as my mana bar filled. "We blew my budget for the week already. I'm going to have to sell some of the stuff from the auction if we want to eat. Maybe that book—"

"Your spell book? I wouldn't recommend that," Lily said.

I looked at where the book had been discarded, the book no longer mundane but glowing with a faint blue light. I picked it up and noticed the pages were filled with words and diagrams, all written in a tight cursive script that hadn't been there before.

"This... where did this come from?" I muttered.

"It's always been there. You just weren't able to see it with your arcane sight inactive."

"I have arcane sight?"

"Yes. The hidden world will be open to you now. Look at the briefcase."

Faded runes crisscrossed the briefcase, covering every inch of the leather. Strangely enough, I understood some of the runes now— unearned knowledge of individual parts of an alphabet—even if I did not understand the words themselves. I popped the briefcase open and stared at its contents, the wooden boxes that had been neatly replaced, the words that I now knew.

"Were these spell components?" I pointed to the empty boxes, the ones whose contents I had thrown into the garbage.

"Yes. You know, we could sell some of those for good money. The squid eggs themselves would be worth a lot to the right alchemist," Lily said.

"Won't they have dried out?" I frowned and then stopped as knowledge of the runes flowed into my mind. "Preservation runes. But won't I need them?"

"Not at all. Those are for hedge mages. They need the components to jumpstart their spells. The magic you know bypasses that."

"Huh. Cool," I said as I put the book and the rest of the boxes away. Well, I didn't know any alchemists, so selling the spell components was pointless. Instead, I pushed the briefcase aside and proceeded to bundle a bunch of clothing together before I tossed it into a garbage bag. "Okay, time to go."

"Where are we going?" Lily said, suddenly looking excited.

"Nora's. Now, come on."

Chapter 3

I squinted slightly as I walked into the sunlight, my eyes adjusting to the brightness. Midsummer, we had a ton of time before the sun set, but not so much before Nora's was closed. Beside me, Lily looked around with wide eyes as she took in the city. In the distance, skyscrapers reached for space, metal fingers stabbing into the bottom of the blue sky. Cars drove past, sharing space with bicycles and motorcycles, the constant rumble of the city assaulting our ears. As I moved to step forward, Lily grabbed my arm, holding me back as she continued to take in the changed world.

"Sorry. Just a lot to take in," Lily muttered, and I nodded.

The same for me as well. I realized the world had changed a little since I had last come outside. A small apartment building glowed with arcane runes, and farther down the road, gargoyles that were once decorative moved as they looked at us. As a pedestrian strode pass me, my jaw dropped when I realized she was a lizardwoman, scales running along her face and along her wide body. Down the street, a humanoid dog creature scurried down the street followed by its larger, fur-covered handler. "What is all this?"

"The hidden world," Lily said. "Your sight is letting you see what was there before, hidden by glamours and spells."

"How do I turn it off?" I muttered, shaking my head. "I mean, how do I know what they're trying to show me?"

"Let your eyes unfocus a bit, look slightly away from them. Use your peripheral vision," Lily coached, and I focused on the dog creature and his handler. I struggled for a few seconds before I learned the trick, unfocusing my eyes to see the glamour. For a second, I saw what they were showing the world—a child and his father—rather than what they were.

"Huh," I said. I turned to Lily, but the raven-haired jinn looked the same no matter how I squinted, unfocused my eyes, or looked away. I only stopped when I realized that passersby were giving me strange looks and starting to walk wide around us.

"Don't bother. You can't break through my glamor yet, though you'll get better with practice and higher levels," Lily explained.

I turned away from her then to practice further. Lily nudged me, and I turned away from the eight-foot-tall giant I had been staring at and started the thirty-minute walk to Nora's, my bag slung over my shoulder.

***

The walk to Nora's took longer than normal, and I had to switch the bag in my hand a couple of times. Both Lily and I stared about us as we walked, the jinn asking questions about the modern world and I about the hidden. Smartphones, elves, earbuds, and alchemical potions—all were queried and explained. At the end of the walk, I wasn't sure who was more awe-filled.

I stood outside the used consignment shop and noticed a series of runic carvings along the door, glowing with the light blue that I'd come to recognize as an active enchantment, that curled around the simple sign saying "Nora's." I unfocused my eyes for a moment and saw the plain old store I had visited dozens of times. For a moment, I hesitated, but in the end, I stepped in. I needed the money.

"El?" I called as I stepped in, the bell ringing as the door swung open.

"Hey, Henry…" El's voice trailed off as a person looked at me, her eyes wide.

A second later, as Lily stepped into the store and passed the runes, the entire room glowed red. The shop woman's eyes narrowed, focused on the raven-haired jinn.

"Who are you?" I stared at the person who had El's voice. Gone was the friendly five-foot, black-haired, and slightly dumpy shopkeeper, and instead, a slim, flame-red-haired beauty with long, pointed ears stood in her place. As I unfocused my eyes, I realized that this was El, as she truly was. "El…?"

"You became a wizard," El said, her tone disappointed. "Did you use her to do it? Did you make a deal with one of them?"

"What are you?" I said, shaking my head and ignoring her questions.

"Pixie. She's a pixie," Lily said, sauntering to the counter and leaning on it. The jinn let her gaze wander around the shop, eyeing the runic enchantments that lined the walls and the glowing glass cases that were always locked. "And this is not just a used clothing store."

"What do you want, demon?" El's hand came out from under the counter, carrying a wand. Even inexperienced as I was, I could guess it wasn't for turning pumpkins into coaches. Though she might try turning Lily into a rat.

"Nothing. I'm just along for the ride," Lily said, and El growled as she lifted the wand.

"Not that kind of ride!" I hastily added and stepped forward. "And Lily's no demon. She's a jinn. And I didn't make a deal. I made a wish."

"Toe-may-toe, toh-mah-toh," El said. Still, the words I'd said seemed to calm El down slightly, her gaze straying to my hand, where the ring rested. "Wishes with a jinn never go well."

"El, all I'm looking for is to sell some clothes. I didn't expect..." I waved my hands to encompass everything.

"Henry, you're a nice boy. So, here's a piece of advice. If you've got a wish left, wish for things to go back to the way they were before," El said.

"Actually, that's a horrible wish," Lily cut in, shaking her head. "Altering time is impossible, so

I'd have to take away your gifts without taking away all the knowledge you have."

El frowned as she stared at Lily while I dropped the clothing bag on the counter. I coughed and drew her attention back to me. "Look, El, I really need your help. Ms. Never-Ending Stomach here ate through all my food and blew my budget. She even found my three-year-old cans of Spam."

"How long have you been living with her?" El said, her head tilted to the side.

"Ummm… a day and a half?" I sighed. "Come on, El, you know I don't bring junk."

"Henry," El sighed and waved at the clothes. "Have you ever looked at the prices I sell the clothes you bring me?"

"Noooo."

"I barely make any money on the clothing I sell. The entire used clothing side is a sham, a front," El said and waved a hand to the glass cases. "That's where I make my money."

"Okay. That's fine, but…" I pointed to the clothing. "Can't you take it as usual?"

"No. Because you're in my world now," El insisted, and I grunted, deflating.

"Fine." I started packing the bag again. Second Chance was a bus ride away and would probably only take a third of my inventory, but at least we'd have enough for dinner. "What do you sell anyway?"

"Spell and runic components," El said.

I choked, staring at the diminutive pixie. As casually as I could, I added, "And do you buy those too?"

El laughed, nodding her head. "Of course. But the careful sorting and care for spell components is a skill. Capturing the first breath of sunlight, containing the sap of a necrotic beetle, it's not something you can just do."

Lily beside me just grinned, and I finished stuffing the clothes away.

"Right. Right. Thank you, El. See you soon."

Outside the door, I turned to Lily, who chuckled quietly beside me. After a few yards, Lily asked, "Isn't the basement the other way?"

"Yes. But I've still got a bag of clothing to get rid of," I replied, hefting it.

"You do know that a single spell component is worth more than ten of those bags of used clothing?" Lily said.

"How would you know?" I shot back. "You've been stuck in a ring."

"I was looking at the clothing," Lily said. "And even at full price, a spell component is worth ten bags. At least."

"Whatever. I still have to get rid of this." I hefted the bag. "Waste not, want not."

***

It was nearly late evening before we found ourselves back at El's door. The titular Nora was, of course, not around, but El was still inside, finishing up for the day. I frowned—tempted to not knock—but decided to do so anyway. It had been a long, long day already, and I just wanted this done. Beside me, Lily was eating a shawarma, her foot tapping on the ground impatiently.

"We really should be home," Lily said. "You're not really ready for nighttime yet."

"Yeah, yeah," I muttered and knocked again.

El finally opened the door, glaring at the pair of us. "What do you want?"

"I might have something you want," I said.

"Henry—"

I shook my head. "Not clothes," I replied immediately. I quickly glanced around, then reached into my jacket and pulled out one of the rune-covered boxes. "A spell component."

"Where did you—?" El clamped her mouth shut. "Fine. Come in."

A few minutes later, we were hunched over a table in the back of the shop, in a room I had never seen before. In the center of the table, the opened enchanted box dominated our conversation, El lifting and placing aside small green crystals with a tweezer, inspecting each piece as it came out.

"Where did you get this?" El muttered, shaking her head. "I haven't seen quality like this in years."

"So, you can give us a good price?" I said, almost bouncing with anticipation.

"Definitely," El said and then clamped her lips shut, a look of frustration flickering on her face.

"Damn it, Henry. I've been buying clothing from you too much."

I chuckled and sat back while she carefully stored them away in a glass container of her own. Once she had finished, she weighed the container before turning back to me. "Would you sell the box too?"

Out of the corner of my eyes, I saw Lily shake her head no, but I did not require her advice on that. I had no intention of selling the boxes and told El as much. The pixie ran a hand through her red hair before she pushed the pad forward, showing me her offer.

"Whoa…" My jaw dropped a bit, staring at the price. Ten times what I had earned this was not. Obviously, Lily's time in the ring had seen more changes than the jinn had expected.

"I take it this is agreeable," El said with a smirk, and I could only nod dumbly.

***

Outside Nora's, lighter one spell component and a newly counted wad of cash stuffed in my pocket, I turned and started the walk back to my basement apartment. Lily fell in beside me, eyeing shops with interest and muttering about supper. It was no surprise I never saw the hand that reached out of the alleyway and yanked me in, dazed by the new hidden world and my newfound wealth.

A large, green, and rough hand gripped me and dragged me deep into the alleyway, holding me by my jacket as I scrabbled at it, trying to make it release me. In the dark, my attacker slammed me into the wall once and then again, sending stars dancing in my eyes while a second hand pinned my right hand to the wall.

"Give me what you bought, Wizard," snarled the green, tusked face inches from mine. To punctuate his words, the orc squeezed my neck, making me choke.

I slapped at his hand ineffectually with my left hand, stars still dancing in my eyes. The repeated blows and lack of oxygen made my eyes unfocus, and for a moment, I saw the hulking skinhead that he showed the rest of the world.

"You know, he can't answer you if he can't breathe," Lily said.

The orc blinked, turning to stare at the jinn who was standing and watching us indifferently. Beside her, a pair of his associates floated in the air, their limbs failing to find purchase.

"You're a wizard too!" the orc growled, yellow eyes narrowing.

He reached a hand backward but stopped when Lily tsked.

"No, no. I'm not your target. He is," Lily said, pointing to me. "Now, this is a decent random encounter but not level appropriate with all three of you, so I'm taking your friends out of the equation. You, Henry will have to deal with. Isn't that right, Henry?"

I didn't get in fights as a matter of course. That being said, it didn't mean I hadn't been in fights before. One of the main rules: don't get distracted, and if your opponent does, capitalize. A raggedly drawn breath gave me enough clarity to focus and cast my only offensive spell with my free hand. I swirled my hand, fingers dancing, before I jabbed it into his chest, the glowing ball of force smashing into my mugger's short ribs.

Force Bolt Cast
Synchronicity 41%

Force Bolt does 9 damage to Orc Mugger.

The surprise attack cracked bone and forced the orc to exhale a surprisingly minty breath into my face, and he reflexively released my neck. Now on my knees, I tackled the orc even though he was clearly heavier than me, my shoulder striking his broken ribs and driving the monster back. Reflexive motion made him hunch over, which gave me the perfect setup for an elbow to his chin. I pushed away from him, giving myself space as I shook my arm out, elbow aching from the strike.

"You know, you're a mage now," Lily said casually. "No experience for slugging it out."

I growled in response and then coughed, choking from the newly formed bruises on my neck. The orc stood up, rubbing his chin, a glimmer of respect in his eyes.

"A wizard with some physical skill," the orc said, his voice a low growl. He flicked a glance to Lily, who waved her hand for him to continue. "This might just be interesting."

"Yeah… no," I said, my right hand darting and twisting as I formed another Force Bolt. Before I could finish, the orc charged me, which forced me to dance backward and interrupt the spell. I twisted and turned as my mugger refused to give me time to finish it. Again and again, I would start the spell before I found it interrupted.

"You're going to have to learn to cast under pressure," Lily coached from the sidelines. A thrown knife from one of the other orcs hung suspended in midair, stopped the moment it had been released from his hand, its target Lily. "Don't let his attacks distract you. The spell is the most important thing."

A fist glanced off my jaw and sent me sprawling to the ground. The orc dashed forward, but I raised my feet high, holding the creature off with my feet. As the monster tried to get to me, I started casting Force Bolt again even as my head throbbed. Two seconds was all the time I would need. Even as the orc finally pushed my legs aside, I finally completed the spell and sent it hammering into the monster.

Force Bolt Cast

Synchronicity 53%

Force Bolt does 10 damage to Orc Mugger.

On my back, feet up in the air, I formed the next spell, which the mugger dodged. Two more spells followed, cast from my back, only one of which hit. My head continued to throb. The pain grew, and I spared a glance upward to note that my mana was nearly gone. All those failed attempts had required mana even if I hadn't completed them.

The orc, arm clutched where it had taken the blunt of the last spell, growled at me. I had heard the crack of another broken bone, but he was still on his feet. Still, the mugger did not attempt to rush me anymore, and I slowly stood up, keeping a distance from it.

"We done?" I asked, trying to keep my voice confident.

"Wizard, I am disappointed. You have some skill. Why do you refuse to fight honorably?" The orc growled and eyed me warily.

"Got to level up."

"You speak strangely even for a wizard."

"Yeah, yeah. We continuing this, or are we done?" I growled, my hand raised as I bluffed the monster.

"We are done if you will have it so, Wizard."

"Go."

"I am Ulrik of the Yellow Eyes," the orc said. "You shall not be as fortunate in our next encounter."

I waved Ulrik away, and Lily let the pair of orcs drop. The trio scrambled off as they eyed the jinn warily. In moments, Lily and I were alone in the alleyway.

"Thanks for all the help," I grumbled at her.

"You need to level up. I made sure it was level appropriate," Lily said unapologetically. "That technique was less than orthodox. Effective though."

"So, did I get experience for that, or did I need to kill him?" I asked as I leaned against the wall and held my hand to my throbbing head.

"What did I say about experience? It's about learning and growing your magical strength, not your ability to kill monsters. Look at your sheet."

Class: Mage
Level 1 (48% Experience)
Known Spells: Light Ball, Force Bolt, Warmth, Chill, Chime, Breeze

"All that from one fight?" I said as I stared at the updated sheet.

"No. You gained some experience while walking around with your arcane sight today. But a lot of it did come from the fight."

I slowly nodded, somewhat mollified. Although I was bruised, headache or not, the random encounter had been worth it. "Fine."

"So, I've got an important question," Lily said, smiling as she walked forward. "Is that Ethiopian restaurant any good?"

Chapter 4

The answer to that important question was no. Very much no. That did not stop Lily from finishing it all while she hogged my computer. Funnily enough, I did not mind it as much as I spent my time poring over the spell book I had acquired. Most of it was unintelligible, series of arcane words and concepts that I had no basis of understanding, but some of it made sense. It was like reading a post-graduate textbook on physics and only having a grade-school education. Still, I persisted.

As I sat reading, I realized my mana was recharging, albeit slowly. Too slowly for my liking. "Lily, is there a way to recharge mana faster?"

"Of course. Certain tonics, foods, and alchemical potions are the most common. Staying in ley lines or nodes will help," Lily said, not bothering to look up. "Meditating, of course."

I nodded slowly and closed the book. Well, okay then. We might not have given me any skills, but grade-school lessons on mindfulness might still help. As I crossed my legs on the bed, I slowed my breathing and tried to clear my mind. Not surprisingly, it was a lot harder than the last few times I had done this. The last days had been somewhat hectic—a jinn, magic, a hidden world, and an old friend not being who I'd thought she was. And then, the first fight I'd been part of for years.

In time, I found my thoughts slowing, relaxing. My eyes closed, my breathing slowed, and then darkness came.

***

"Morning," Lily greeted, along with the enticing smell of fried bacon, tomatoes, scrambled eggs, and the nectar of the gods—coffee. The jinn stood over the stove as she finished plating the meal. Hair left unbound, the raven-haired jinn was bent over in a pink blouse, a flowered vest, and a pair of tight blue jeans that looked uncannily familiar. Doing mundane tasks like this, I could almost think of the jinn as just another gorgeous woman and not a powerful supernatural creature.

"Breakfast?" I swung my feet off the bed and wandered over to snag a plate from the counter. Used plates piled high reminded me that I really needed to do the dishes. "Are those clothes from El's store?"

"I copied some of them for use. Your wardrobe is less than fashionable," Lily said, shaking her head. "Really? A dozen shirts about this *Firefly* thing?"

"Don't knock it till you've seen it," I muttered around a mouthful of food. "So, what now? I wander around the city looking for trouble?"

"No. I've got a quest for you." Lily waved her fork at my desk. It took me a few minutes of searching through the scattered papers before I found the right one. On it, circled in red ink, was "Quest One."

"Rats?" I poked at the paper as I walked to get more coffee.

"Rats. It's tradition."

"You are kidding me," I grumbled and sipped my coffee. "Also, what did you do to the coffee? It's really smooth."

"Cold brew," Lily said. "Your coffee maker is pitiful. And I'm not. Devil Rats should be perfect for your first quest. Level appropriate."

"How do you know these are Devil Rats though? The news report just talks of an increase in disappearances of pets in the neighborhood," I said. "Might be coyotes."

Lily shook her head. "GM. I expanded a bit of my power to check our surroundings. Now, off you go to kill some rats. Though maybe a shower first?"

I growled softly before I walked to the bathroom. Now, the real question was, what do you wear when you go hunting supernatural rats in the sewer?

***

It took a bit of hunting, but I found a pair of rubber boots, wool socks, and workout pants along with one of my faded shirts. A simple polyester rain jacket to keep the cold and wet out and I was ready to go. Or as ready as I could be considering I had no idea what I was getting into.

An underground train ride and a bus ride later, I found myself in the Devil Rat-plagued suburban neighborhood. I never understood how people could live out in these cookie-cutter houses with their carefully manicured lawns and nosy neighbors. Every time I came out here, I was reminded how stale and artificial it all felt, a residence made by design rather than need, a place to rest and hide away from the world.

As I walked away from the bus stop, I eyed the ground, searching for a manhole cover. It was only when I found one in a deserted cul-de-sac and attempted to pull it open that I realized one flaw with my plan—my lack of upper-arm strength and leverage. A few minutes of futile gripping and straining later, I sat down beside the manhole cover and applied some brainpower to the problem. Perhaps…

I held my hand over the manhole cover, focusing not on my hand but slightly past it. I focused deep within and cast the spell, altering the flows slightly so that instead of forming right at my hand and shooting outward, the spell would form beneath the cover. Three failed attempts later, the spell finally formed, and the Force Bolt crashed into the underside of the obstruction, tossing it into the air by a few inches.

"Owwww," I muttered as I carefully levered the manhole off my foot, which I had shoved into the opening. That was going to leave a bruise. Right. Crowbars. Definitely adding a crowbar to my adventuring kit.

I left the manhole propped mostly open and climbed down to the sewers, finally ready to complete my quest. At least the hard part was over. How hard could rats be?

***

"Force Bolt in your face, Mickey!" I snarled as my spell finished forming and smashed the Devil Rat aside. Crushed under the blue bolt of arcane energy, the splattered remains of my attacker left a red smear against the grey walls of the sewer tunnel. Above me, a floating light orb—that I had figured how to tether to my body—gave off fitful light, casting shadows all around. Thankfully, the sewer system that was connected to this suburban zone was actually part of the flood water preparations, so the sewer itself was tall and wide to accommodate a large amount of water. It meant that I could, for the most part, stand upright while hunting around.

I slumped against the wall and dug into my backpack, searching for the bandages I had thoughtfully brought along. A dose of iodine later, I wrapped my injured calf tightly and hoped Devil Rats were not as plague-ridden as their mundane counterparts. Somehow, I had a feeling that was wishful thinking.

"Good thing Lily isn't here to see this," I said to myself. I imagined the jinn smirking while I struggled to fight Devil Rats in the dark. In truth, I wasn't sure what I had expected for this quest. She'd said this was level appropriate, and my previous life as a retail store worker and part-time bargain hunter had done little to ready me for monster hunting. I looked sideways, eyeing my mana bar, which stood a quarter full. Enough for one more fight.

With quick motions, I put away my first aid kit and stood, testing my foot and finding it sound enough. That it had to be same foot I'd bruised earlier made walking even harder than before, but not impossible. As I rounded the next corner of the damp, noxious sewers, I made sure not to think about what I was walking in. Thankfully, years of babysitting for uncles and aunts for extra money had inured me to the concept of feces as a whole, even if wading through the sewers tested the limits of my attitude.

Another mangled body greeted me as I stepped around a corner, a poodle with its innards scattered, and a Devil Rat poked its head out from within. The fellow in front of me was typical for the Devil Rats I had encountered—the size of a housecat with glowing red eyes and an aggressive temperament. As it arched its back in defense of its meal, I finished my spell and pointed my fingers at it, the bolt catching the monster in the center of its body and crushing its heart.

Force Bolt Cast
Synchronicity 67%

Force Bolt does 11 damage to Devil Rat.

Slumping down to the corpse, I exhaled in relief and tried to get the adrenaline spike under control again. Thankfully, this time, I'd been the one to catch the rat by surprise. The monsters had a tendency to attack from hiding, crawling from dark corners to set upon me. Still, with my mana bar nearly empty, the headache had returned, and so I settled in to wait and rest.

This was not going to be easy.

***

I stood up after a bit, meditating having slowly driven my mana bar to half full. I would have stayed longer, but there were limits to my ability to ignore how disgusting all this was even if my nose had long ago shut off. A low squeaking had taken me down a side corridor, and I was forced to hunch over as I scrabbled forward. A small worm of worry crawled along my guts, the noises before me growing louder and more numerous than I had heard before.

"Oh, shit," I muttered softly as my light finally illuminated the nest before me. Curled up in a pile of bones, rat droppings, and shed fur, a mother rat twice the size of any I'd seen before was nursing a group of Devil Rat pups, each the size of my fist. Crouched near them was another Devil Rat, gnawing on a pale bone. As my light drew their attention, the mischief of rats turned and regarded me with their hellish red eyes. Taking the better part of valor, I started to slowly back away as I readied a Force Bolt.

At first, the rats just regarded my slow retreat without moving. As my light pulled away, the rats started squeaking louder and louder, the noise echoing through the cramped quarters. Mouth dry, I could sense the monsters getting ready to attack as I sloshed backward. Fear clutched at my stomach, knowing I had insufficient mana to kill them all. I needed to make sure when they charged, I had time to do something.

Inspiration struck as I stepped backward. I snapped and twisted my fingers, then pointed down, sending arcane energy into the water as I chilled it in front of me and backed away. Within seconds, a light crust of ice formed on the water, spreading faster and faster as the arcane energy drew heat from the already chilly water. As if my magic was the signal, there was a sudden silence as the rats barreled forward.

I scrambled backward as I poured mana into the water, creating a slick surface that the first Devil Rat hit without warning. Front claws dug into the slick, wet ice, sending it spinning and twisting to slam into the wall. The rat shook its head to clear it while the pups, unsteady on their feet, skidded and scattered on my impromptu ice rink.

As a spike of pain erupted in my head, I stopped the spell, unable to continue, and backed away as fast as I could. Once out of the small tunnel, I turned and ran, the sounds of the larger mother rat crashing into and crushing my ice echoing through the tunnel.

I never looked back, running as fast as I could to the nearest ladder and climbing as quickly as possible. I hit the manhole cover with my shoulder, adrenaline and better leverage allowing me to push it upward. Outside, the feel of sunlight on my face and the smell of blooming flowers carried on the wind blew away some of my fear, some of the nightmare-inducing madness below. As I replaced the manhole cover, I flashed a smile at a child playing on the sidewalk, grateful to have survived my first quest.

Chapter 5

Extra clothing. That was what I'd forgotten to bring with me. That was clear as I sat in my own smelly sphere on the ride back. I kept my face down in embarrassment as other passengers threw disgusted looks at me, even those from the hidden world. By the time I made my way back, that lesson had been deeply ingrained into my soul. Always bring extra clothing.

Lily was crouched in front of my laptop when I came back, clicking away and killing virtual monsters the entire time I had been dealing with real ones. Rather than speak with my titular GM, I stalked into the bathroom to shower and clean up as best I could. Leaden silence carried through the air as I walked out in a fresh set of clothing and began to cook dinner.

It was only when dinner was served that I spoke, my voice tight and controlled. "So, I killed some Devil Rats."

"I'd hope so," Lily said, taking the plate of pork chop, gravy, mashed potatoes, and brussels sprouts from me. "Did you kill the ten rats?"

"No," I said as I stabbed my pork chop and sawed at the piece. "There was a mother rat, about the size of a medium-sized dog, in there."

"Ugly little creature, isn't she?" Lily said, already having walked back to the laptop.

"She nearly killed me. They nearly killed me!" I shouted and then drew a deep breath, forcing myself to calm down. Last night, the orc had been scary, but it had just been a mugging. I'd been mugged before, and while it was never fun, muggers were never really there to kill you. Rough you up a bit, maybe hurt you, but not kill. Not unless things got out of hand. At least, the ones who weren't on drugs. The rats though, the rats didn't care about legal consequences or moral imperatives to not kill. To them, I was just food.

"Of course. You were trying to kill them, weren't you?" Lily sighed and put her cutlery down before she stared at me, my shaking fingers, and my shallow breathing. For a moment, I saw a flash of sympathy before Lily continued. "This is what questing and combat is. High-stress situations that require you to learn and explore your abilities."

I gulped as I stared at my hands that wouldn't stop shaking, at my body that refused to stop shivering. I could not stop thinking about the fact that I had nearly been eaten alive. Of the pain of being bitten and the sharp needlelike teeth.

"It's your choice, Henry. We can continue doing quests like this, or you can stay home, casting spells and learning slowly. You can level up however you want," Lily said softly, but I could barely hear her as I contemplated my mortality.

For the first time, I had an inkling that perhaps learning and wielding magic wasn't just about having a cool trick. There were real consequences here.

***

When I woke the next morning, my wounds had miraculously healed, and there was new, lightly-scarred skin where they had been. I exhaled a sigh of relief, glad we'd managed to get that sorted. Of course, the healing had left me ravenously hungry since all it did was speed the healing process, but I'd take a higher grocery bill over limping for days.

Surprisingly, I found that Lily was not at the laptop when I woke. A very brief check showed the jinn was not in the apartment, which left me staring at the ring. Of course, she could have left the flat entirely. I briefly contemplated rubbing the ring to bring her to me before I shook my head and discarded the idea. Instead, I reveled in the fact that I had my apartment back to myself.

Living as a bachelor for years now, I had forgotten what it was like to have a roommate, the constant presence that intruded on my daily routines. I could lounge about in my underwear. I could watch schlocky TV or just play on my computer. And I did all that, a bowl of instant noodles in hand.

Yet, every few minutes, I found my gaze traveling back to the rubber boots I had so carefully cleaned off last night. Distractions that used to carry me away from my life for hours, even days, on end barely held my attention for minutes now. Even casting a spell felt hollow, an exercise that had no point.

No point… that was the thing, wasn't it? There was no point to this, to my life. It was a malaise I had felt before, that had left me fired from retail jobs when I simply stopped caring. There was no point to this, to TV shows that had no end, computer games that had no challenge, and jobs that had no future. But magic and that quest? At least there I was doing something. I was progressing, making myself better. I had dreamed of having magic all my life, and now I had it. Even if all I was doing was questing and killing monsters, I was progressing.

I stared at my rubber boots sitting accusingly by the door, and finally, I sighed and stood up.

"Fine. Let's do this."

***

Of course, it wasn't that easy. First, I had to find more disposable clothing. At this rate, I'd become a customer of Nora's. A sealed plastic bag contained a second set of clothing while sandwiches and water, a crowbar, a hammer, and an old hunting knife ended up in my bag for later. An extra flashlight and some light sticks were added along with a new roll of bandages. I frowned, trying to decide if I had missed anything, and realized I was just killing time, avoiding the next step.

As I was about to walk out the door, my phone rang. I frowned, fishing it out and staring at the glowing caller ID. I drew a deep breath, feeling my stomach clench even as I answered it.

"Mommy," I greeted.

"When were you going to call?" immediately on the attack, my mother's familiar voice resounded through the phone. I felt my shoulders hunch, my entire body shrinking down slightly at the accusation. Justified. I hadn't spoken with her or my dad in months.

"Soon. Sorry, things have been busy," I answered apologetically.

"You found a new job?" Hope was in her voice even after all these years.

"No. Yes. Sort of," I said, unsure of how and whether to explain things. Actually, no. I knew better than to explain.

"Oh." Disappointment now. I wince, knowing once again, I've let her down. As usual—the black sheep of the family, the useless one, especially compared to my doctor sister and accountant brother.

"It's a part-time thing," I clarified, figuring that was true enough at least. "Anyway... I was just about to head out…"

"I wanted to ask, are you coming back for your father's birthday? You know he'd like it."

"I don't know," I answered truthfully. I really didn't want to go back, to travel hundreds of miles to be subjected to passive-aggressive stares and the constant looks of disappointment. It was why I had left Vancouver after all.

"Do you need money? I can send you some."

"I can pay for it. It's just a new job…" I explained hurriedly and then glanced at the door again. "I really need to get going…"

"Fine. Just remember to call and tell us."

"I will. It's not for months yet!" I said. "Bye!" I hurriedly finished the exchange of pleasantries before I finally ended the call, my stomach aching with phantom pain. Stupid family. Pushing aside the never-ending drama, I left the apartment.

A train and bus ride later, I was back at the suburb. I checked my phone and its GPS tracking of where I'd been—which, by the way, was sort of creepy—and I was at the manhole cover I had crawled out of the previous day. Unlike the first one I'd entered, this manhole cover was in the middle of the street, but at this point, I was more than done with being circumspect. A crowbar and an almost-strained back later, I was back in the nightmare-inducing darkness.

"Light," I muttered as I cast my spell. A vocal component was not required, but one aspect that I knew of this magic was that "required" did not equal "not important." I wasn't entirely sure if it was the addition of a vocal rhythm or the addition of a vocal aspect itself, but the results certainly showed up.

Light Ball Cast
93% Synchronicity

As an added precaution, I popped a glow stick and zip-tied it to the ladder. Nose scrunched from the smell, I stood at the ladder and listened, trying to discern if I had a greeting party. Hearing nothing, I slowly approached the corridor that I had exited so ignobly a day ago.

As I walked, I wiped sweaty palms against my sweatpants and swallowed around the copper taste of adrenaline in my mouth. In my left hand, I hefted my crowbar, ready to ward off a Devil Rat while my right readied itself to cast a Force Bolt. At the mouth of the corridor, I raised my hand and cast another Light Ball, this time in silence, and directed it to the edges of my current illuminated area. Again and again, I did so, lighting the entire corridor till the excited squeals of Devil Rats alerted to my presence reached my ears.

The first adult Devil Rat exploded from the shadows and rushed me, closely followed by another. Right behind, the pups raced to catch their larger, faster brethren. From my hand, a Force Bolt flew out to strike the lead Devil Rat. The Force Bolt crushed the monster's front legs, causing it to fall and mewl pitifully. No longer a threat, I turned to the next adult rat.

Seconds had passed, and the monster was already halfway to me, the pups only a short distance behind. I snarled as my second Force Bolt passed by uselessly, the third injuring but not killing the monster. Too close for a follow-up spell, I instead swung the crowbar and battered the attacker away, blood and brain matter spattering around me at my successful strike.

And then it was the rats' turn as the pups swarmed me. The next few seconds were a blur as I swung, punched, kicked, and stomped at the tiny monsters that crawled, bit, and tore at me. I had no time for spells, no time but the dance for survival. But monsters or not, they were only the size of normal rats. One after another, the monsters fell before my weapon and stomping feet before a searing pain ripped into my calf.

I fell to the ground, the mother rat clamped onto my ankle and refusing to let go. Each movement tore the wound open wider. In pain, I raised my crowbar to swing at it, but a last pup bit into the edges of my triceps. My hand spasmed open, and I screamed again.

The mother rat twisted its head one last time and tore my calf open before it backed off and lunged toward my torso. Its teeth clamped onto my hip, sharp teeth tearing into the tender flesh. I thrashed on the ground, a wild swing batting away the last pup and driving the mom aside.

"Die!" I scowled as I tried to scurry away and twisted, my injured foot swinging at the monster.

Teeth clamped onto my boot, sharp teeth unable to penetrate the rubber immediately. My hand twisted and pointed, and a Force Bolt flew forward at the enraged monster.

"Aaarggh!" I screamed, the spell tearing the mother Devil Rat away as the bolt impacted my foot and the rat. Bones cracked under the impact of the spell, pain making my eyes widen. The mother rat, its teeth missing from when it was ripped away and its mouth bloody, rushed me once more. I shoved my hand forward, fingers dancing faster than ever, and I sent the spell into its open mouth as it lunged for my neck.

The Force Bolt tore down its throat and tore it apart as it threw her back. Blood sprayed and aerosoled as the creature fell to the ground, dead but still twitching. I coughed, throat sore and dry from screaming as blood dripped from my wounds.

Blood, so much blood. I grunted, struggling to pull my bag out from under me. Its contents were soaked by sewer water, but thankfully, the first aid bag was waterproof. As my fingers shook, I slowly pulled my first aid gear from my bag and began the long and painful process of cleaning my wounds.

***

The trip back this time was less of a social issue as wet wipes and a new set of clothing made me look and smell less like a hobo. It didn't hide the way I moved or the pain that flashed across my face, but no one bothered me at least. The lack of public embarrassment unfortunately left me more time to consider the waves of pain that rose and fell with each bump and step on the journey home.

Two blocks from the train station to my house, and for some reason, I was drawing looks again. I smiled and nodded, too tired to answer queries about my health as the world begin to shimmer before my eyes.

"I see you. And I got a Force Bolt for you if needed," I said to the gargoyle who shifted to stare at me when I walked past its perch.

Descending the stairs, each step forced me to draw a deep breath as I squelched down. I pushed on the handle, opening the door, and I stumbled in and waved my hand triumphantly into the empty space. "The conquering hero returns!"

The bed, a bare five feet from the door greeted me as I flopped onto it, darkness finally claiming me.

Chapter 6

I woke up groggy, mouth dry, and shivering. My shirt was stained with sweat, and as I rolled over, I saw Lily seated beside me on the computer. When I shifted, the jinn looked at me and broke into a smile, helping me sit up to drink a cup of water and wash down some painkillers. Unlike last time I slept and healed, my calf ached, throbbing in pain with each heartbeat.

"What…?" I growled, shaking my head, and poked at my foot. "Why didn't it heal?"

"Whoever did that carried a magical disease. The enhanced healing I gave you can't remove it," Lily explained.

"Can you heal it?" I asked, and she shook her head, crossing her hands together as if they were tied. Right. Right. Not allowed to interfere. I guessed taking my boots off and cleaning me up wasn't considered undue interference though. Or taking off my pants. I flushed red, the increase in blood flow making me dizzy for a second. Or it could have been the fever.

"Henry?" Lily asked, placing a hand on my arm. "You need help. Magical help."

I nodded dumbly and stared at the phone the jinn was pointedly looking at. Right. Phone. Help. Except I didn't know anyone magical except Lily. I slumped back against my pillows, my eyes half closing. A sudden scream jerked me awake, making me stare at the computer where Lily's avatar had died gruesomely down a pit.

"Don't fall asleep just yet. You need to call for help."

Help. Right. I took hold of the phone, getting as far as 9-1-1 before I canceled the call. Magical help. For a moment, I stared at the ceiling, wondering why everyone always painted their ceilings a boring white. They should have colored them something more interesting, something fun. Vibrant. Red. Red like El's hair…

Holding on to that thread of thought, I scrolled to the shop's number and hit dial, then listened to the insistent ring.

"Nora's, your everyday used clothing store. El speaking."

"Henry speaking," I said and grinned at my reply.

"Henry, what can I do for you?"

"Nothing. No. Not nothing. I had something…" I frowned, trying to remember why I called her. It was funny, the way the raven-haired jinn's face was screwed up as she listened to me on the phone. "Oh, I love your hair. Your real hair. It's so much more you."

"Was that all you called me for?" El said, her voice sounding tinny over the phone.

"Yes. It's pretty. Just like you." I smiled and killed the call, happy that I'd remembered what I had done. The phone dropped from my hand, landing on the edge of the bed and bouncing off. Bounce, bounce. That looked fun, so I let myself drop too and bounced on the bed before my eyes closed.

***

"What did you do to him, Jinn!" I heard El's voice in the distance.

"Nothing, you crazed pixie. I was the one who told him to call you!"

Screams and shouts, the crackle of electricity, and then silence.

***

"Oh, Henry. You idiot," El said, as my eyes opened. My dumpy friend, clad in her featureless gray sweater swapped with an elfin apparition clad in green and brown. Hands held over my leg streamed color, arcane energy that I could now see chasing away the cold that had wrapped my leg. Warmth filled it for the first time in what seemed like ages.

Then pain.

I screamed, strong hands holding me down.

"Hold him still!"

"I'm trying, but I can't do too much. I told you we should have strapped him down!" This time, Lily's voice came from a creature of flame and smoke, clawed hands and stunning beauty that made me want to cry intermixing with my jinn, the raven-haired beauty.

Another blast of power came with pain and darkness.

***

I woke slowly this time, free from pain but dry-mouthed. I slowly sat up with a muted groan, brought a nearby cup of water to my lips, and noticed El's concerned face. I sipped at first and then gulped, greedily drinking all the water and asking for more. After the second cup, I pushed up against the bed to see Lily at the laptop, focused on her game.

"What are you doing here, El?" I finally asked. Thankfully, I seemed to be half-dressed at least. Though who had put the fresh pair of boxer briefs on me I refused to consider.

"Your call had me worried. Especially when you didn't answer. Who knows what kind of trouble you could have gotten mixed up with, especially since you have her." El nodded to Lily who stuck her tongue out without looking up. "So, I came over."

"Oh…" I frowned and touched my lower leg. No pain. Not even when I flexed my ankle. "Did you?"

"Heal you? Yes," El answered before shrugging. "Pixies have a modicum of healing magic. Now, stand up. I want to check you out."

Ignoring my initial protests and my embarrassment, the flame-haired pixie got me on my feet. For the next few minutes, El made me stand, bend, stretch, and twist as she tested my newly healed body. Finally satisfied, she had me sit at the dining table where she piled food, carefully heated in the oven, and commanded me to eat. Lily, drawn to the table, received a glare but no other admonishment from El as she dug in as well.

Any attempt at further conversation was shot down till I had stuffed myself. As I pushed away my plate, El raised a finger and said slowly and menacingly, "Now, tell me what happened. All of it."

I shivered, staring at the tiny pixie, the flint in her eyes reminding me of the one time a shoplifter had tried to get away from the store. The look she'd given him then was similar to the one she offered me now and just as effective. I spilled the details of my quest, both the failed first attempt and the second. Lily kept uncharacteristically silent through the tale, the clinking of her fork the only other noise in the apartment. Which, I had quietly noted, had a few new holes in it.

"Men." El huffed when I finished, rolling her eyes to the sky with her arms crossed. "You almost got yourself killed because of a... quest?"

I paused, giving the question actual thought. In the end, I answered her slowly. "It wasn't the quest itself. Not really. It was the decision. To stay at home training slowly or go out and do something. Anything. If I didn't make it, then, well, it was as good as having made it. You understand?"

"No."

Lily smiled slightly as El glared at me with her arms crossed over her petite breasts. Leaning forward, Lily brought the attention to her as she spoke finally. "Well, that was nice. Don't let the door hit you on the way out."

"Why, you…" El snarled.

"Lily! Stop it. She's my friend, and you need to show her some respect," I snapped at Lily.

"That little tree fairy? Do you know what she did while you were sick?" Lily spluttered, and I shook my head.

"I don't care. She's my friend, and you're going to be respectful to her, or else you can just stay in the ring when she's around," I said, glaring at Lily who returned my glare. We locked gazes for a long while before the jinn broke away, laughing softly.

"Fine, fine. I'll be nice to the… to El," Lily said. "But I do need to speak with you. Alone."

"Not happening," El said.

"This isn't for you, pixie," Lily snapped, and I sighed.

"What's this about?" I asked Lily who mouthed the word "quest" at me. Oh. I'd finished a quest which meant…

Class: Mage
Level 1 (208% Experience)
Known Spells: Light Ball, Force Bolt, Warmth, Chill, Chime, Breeze

"Nice. I can level up!" I exclaimed, and Lily winced, shaking her head.

"Level up?" El's eyes narrowed at the two of us suspiciously.

"My wish—"

"Henry!" Lily snapped at me, leaning forward. "Ixnay on the ishway."

"Oh, come on, Lily. El just saved my life. I think we can trust her," I said, which caused El to flush slightly and Lily to glare at me more. "It's my secret."

"Aaargh!" Lily threw her hands up in the air and then fell silent, which I took for tacit agreement.

"I wanted to be a mage, but I didn't want my brain dribbling out. So, I made a wish that gave me magic but would only pass the spells on in dribs and drabs as I learned to handle it. We based it off, well…" I hesitated, waving my hands to my books.

"Your role-playing games. I get it," El said, rubbing her temples. "It is the most idiotic and—"

"Genius plan ever," Lily finished, nodding firmly. "I know, right? It bypasses most of the problems wishes for magic power have and doesn't stunt his growth. Much."

"Much?" I frowned at Lily.

"She speaks of the Mage Council. They are unlikely to be impressed by your abilities," El clarified. "The jinn is right. You should not have told me this. You should not be telling anyone this."

I blinked and then flashed El my patented Smile No. 3, the one that made me look like a kid. Okay, it was my usual smile, but it still normally worked. "But you won't tell anyone, right?"

"Oh, Henry," El said exasperatedly. "I won't. Just… stop being so damn trusting. The hidden world isn't the same as your mundane one. You cannot just do things like this."

"Okay, okay. I promise. No more telling secrets," I said, crossing my heart and flashing another grin. El just rolled her eyes while I turned to Lily. "So, level up time?"

"Yes. Hold still please. This should hurt less than the last time," Lily said consolingly, and that was when I remembered how much it had hurt.

Oh, hell.

***

"That wasn't bad," I said as I rubbed blood from my nose and gratefully accepted the painkillers from El, who had a strange look on her face.

"Next time, do it on the bed," El said, and I nodded firmly. Passing out at the dinner table and cracking my nose on the table had been a less-than-pleasant experience.

"I hear kitchen tables are quite popular," Lily said, and El flushed, looking away.

"Wait. Did you make a sex joke?" I said before I shook my head. "Never mind. I don't want to know. Now, I'm just going to see what you downloaded."

"Downloaded?" Lily said, puzzled.

I tuned them out as El explained more current lingo to the jinn and focused inward. First things first, my character sheet.

Class: Mage
Level 3 (8% Experience)
Known Spells: Light Ball, Force Missile, Heat, Freeze, Chime, Breeze, Lesser Shield, Heal, Link, Mend

The first thing I noticed was that many of my existing spells had changed name. A brief consideration showed that I still knew the lesser versions of the spells but had instead learned stronger formulas. Those spells in turn allowed me to alter the spells themselves, giving me more options. As an example, I was pretty sure I could actually cast two Force Bolts now rather than a single Force Missile. Though, controlling both Force Bolts and where they would impact would be a lot trickier.

Light Ball had not upgraded, though the intensity and duration of the spell had grown. It was no real surprise—the light spell was a pretty basic spell, and while variants on it were available, most variations were a matter of power rather than formula. The spells that I had not used or practiced, Chime and Breeze, had not changed at all.

Most interestingly, I now knew four new spells. The first was a defensive spell that layered a thin layer of compressed air and arcane energy in front of me. Intuitively, I knew that practice with both Breeze and Lesser Shield would provide me greater understanding of either. It was not a powerful defensive spell, but considering I had started with none, I was grateful for its presence. Perhaps if I'd had the spell to begin with, I would not have been as injured.

The Heal spell was, sadly, pathetic. From the spell formula that sat in my head, the spell did little more than increase the speed of my healing by a minor amount, and almost all of it focused on a small area. It was a useful spell for removing bruises and slowing, even stopping, bleeding by having the body's natural clotting properties act faster, but it was nothing like a cleric's minor healing spell. On the other hand, it was a channeled spell, with the amount of healing dependent on the amount of time it was active. If it wasn't for the fact that I would never progress with healing abilities if I didn't use it, I probably wouldn't even bother casting it at all since resting had a much more powerful effect.

The third spell was the foundation spell for scrying. At this stage, all it really did was highlight links between two objects. The closer their initial sympathetic link, the longer the range of the spell.

Unfortunately, at my level, even a direct connection like blood would only highlight the connection for a few hundred meters. With practice though, the arcane knowledge involved would allow me to scry locations hundreds of miles away. Once I got the appropriate spell, of course.

The last spell was a utility spell, one you didn't see much in role-playing books because throwing around the power of gods was more interesting than fixing a hole in your pants. On the other hand, for a poor gamer like me, the spell could actually save me a few dollars. I even had a few pieces of old electronics sitting around that I kept meaning to throw away properly. Perhaps the spell would fix them?

"Did you learn anything worth your life?" El asked, and I refocused on the pixie, my lip twisting in a half smile.

"Sort of? Some of these spells might keep me alive longer," I said, which caused El to roll her eyes again.

"I have to go. I need to reopen the store," El said finally, standing up and fixing me with a look. "You aren't going to be going out and doing anything stupid, are you?"

"No. Got a whole new bunch of spells in my head. I'll want to test them out first," I replied, and El stared at me in an attempt to ascertain the truth of my words. Good thing I was telling the truth.

"Fine," El said and walked to the door, snatching her coat on the way out. "Just be careful, Henry. You don't understand the world you've entered."

"Roger!" I said, waving goodbye to the pixie.

Lily snorted at our antics, already deep into her game. I stared at the jinn for a second, trying to decide if I had any questions for her that she could answer and found none that were more pressing than testing my new spells.

As I went back to my bed, I rubbed my chin and tried to work out how to test my spells in my six-hundred-square-foot bachelor's apartment without wrecking anything. As I eyed the new holes in the apartment walls, I added "anything more."

****

It turned out that the answer to that question was the bathroom. A pot of water in the bath could steam and boil over without causing damage, and ice, well, a pot of ice really didn't make a difference where you made it. The tricky part, at least for me, was learning how to control the amount of mana I put into the spell. Unlike its lesser variants, which felt like I was pushing beanbags through rabbit holes, the new spells had a hunger for mana like a jinn's stomach.

Between waiting for my mana to recover and poking at the new knowledge in my mind, I found myself walking out of the bathroom to talk to Lily. Questions that hadn't been important till now started creeping into my mind.

***

"That orc called me a wizard, but you call me a mage. What's the difference?"

"Depends on who you ask, but the somewhat official definitions are that mages are trained to use their gifts, normally starting as apprentices. Wizards, on the other hand, are untrained arcane users who have learned to wield their powers via trial and error."

"Any other terms I should know?"

"Sorcerers are generally those who have gained their powers via demonic means. Enchanters are specialized mages—and they're almost always mages—who enchant items and spaces. Alchemists do the same with potions, but they can be wizards too. There are probably more alchemical wizards than mage actually."

"Probably?"

"Things change. And unless I use my powers, it's not as if I have a way of ascertaining what is happening around the world."

"Right."

***

Later, after freezing the pot of ice, I realized instead of a single ice cube, I'd somehow mangled the spell to create ice chunks. Definitely needed to work on the synchronicity for this spell.

"What about this Mage Council?" I asked.

"It's mostly made up of mages, but there are some wizards too. And one sorcerer. Or at least, there was."

"The way I read it, they're not happy with me because I'm cheating the system, learning their secrets from you, and refusing to pay my dues."

"In part." Lily looked up from the laptop. For a moment, her eyes danced with flame while she spoke. "But it's more than that. Past history with jinn and mages has been fraught with tragedy. To be a mage, a powerful mage, you have to be willing to sacrifice everything. The apprenticeship itself takes decades, and apprentices are isolated from all family and friends during their tenure. The weak fall away; only the driven survive."

"And if you're that driven, you're probably not the nicest of people." I rubbed my chin and realized I still hadn't shaved.

"Yes. Most mages know our limitations to some extent. Their wishes are often more circumspect. Still, many die. Those who don't are often driven mad."

"Power-crazy assholes with wishes," I said for her. "And I'm considered one of them. Yay me."

***

86

My spell book was set out in front of me, a window propped open, and the bathroom fan on as we tried to ignore the smell of melted metal and plastic. I was so not going to get my damage deposit back.

"This sort of makes a bit of sense," I muttered as I read the line again. Four out of eleven words. Now, if only those words weren't the arcane equivalents of "and," "but," and "then." Sometimes, I even knew all the words in a sentence. Just not what it meant.

"That's the equivalent of a level-nine spell," Lily said without glancing up, a strand of her hair in her mouth.

"What is it for?"

"You tell me."

"The arcane runes are the same as my Force spell, so it's a Force something. But there's bits of it for distance that don't make sense—there are both distances and limits, height and width definitions." I flipped the page backward and forward, cudgeling my cerebral engine for a few more minutes, and exhaled. "It's a Force Wall."

"Good boy," Lily said and pointed to the book. "Now, back to reading."

I blew my nose again, the melted plastic making my nose run and making me truly uncomfortable as it blended with my mana headache. Ah, the glamour of spellcasting.

***

"You ignorant dung beetle!" Lily snarled at the computer as she banged the mouse against the side table she was using. The noise was sufficient to interrupt the silent contemplation of the spells in my head. The silent, closed-eyed, and very still contemplation of spells.

"Hmmmm…?" I rolled my neck to stare at Lily who pointed at the computer.

"They killed me!"

"So? You've died before. Restart or go back to your last saved game."

"No. Not the game. The players. They killed me! Just outside of town," Lily said, already seated and controlling the mouse.

"What are you playing?" I asked and ambled over to stare at the screen. I groaned quietly as I saw the familiar cartoony images and the half-sized dwarf running along idyllic green hills. "Oh no. You are not pulling anything from that into my wish."

"It's fun!" Lily said and stared at me, eyes narrowed.

"Har! Dozens of expansions in, they've had to nerf everyone constantly and keep adding expansion packs to just keep people interested."

"I bet you wish I'd made you heal like these characters do though!"

I groaned, settling in next to her to argue. Some things you just could not let stand!

"And what's nerf?"

Chapter 7

After my disastrous first quest, El took an active interest in my activities. The next evening, she showed up at my door with an agenda and a refusal to take no for an answer. Lily was not invited on this trip, a fact that the jinn did not seem to mind, other than a request for more shawarma. Over the next hour, I was introduced to the hidden-world denizens of my neighborhood. It seemed that I had, unknowingly, moved into one of the hubs of the supernatural community. While it was not necessarily better, most supernaturals liked to live and work together for convenience. The services and skills they might require—from full-body hair grooming for minotaurs to the specialized diet of dryads—made sense to keep localized.

Before each encounter, El would squeeze my triceps and growl a warning to behave myself, and in just about half the cases, I'd remember not to put my foot in my mouth. The other half generally had me alternating between squeals of geeky fanboyishness and minor eeps of terror, even wide-eyed fear in a few cases.

"Do you think you can hold it together for this next meeting?" El hissed at me as we walked up a staircase.

"It'd help if you told me what I was meeting beforehand," I said.

"Har! You almost ran away when I told you we were about to meet Leda."

"She was a medusa!" I said, my voice rising in protest.

"And the best hairdresser in the city. You nearly cost me my next appointment," El snapped and shook her head. "What? You think if she turned people to stone all the time no one would notice? Leda's kept her secret for years, but she won't if a certain someone keeps shouting about it."

"Sorry. Sorry." I lowered my voice. "You've got to give me a break here. Meeting creatures from myth is kind of out my comfort zone."

"Well, get better. This is your life now," El said as we finally reached the floor. I had to pause for a second to catch my breath before El led us to the correct doorway. Thinking better of it, El added, "Shane's a dwarf."

"Oh…" I relaxed at that. I could deal with dwarves. I mean, vertically-challenged individuals weren't exactly unusual. When the door swung open, I had a smile on my face, all ready to be polite. "GIMLI!"

Oops. But seriously, beyond the fact that Shane was lacking both his armor, axe, and helmet, he could have passed for the famous dwarf. At least as portrayed in the movies—dark-red hair and braided beard of the same color with deep-set eyes and a thoroughly unamused look on his face.

"Shane, this is Henry. He's a newcomer to our world. I've been showing him around a bit," El said after she finished extracting her elbow from my ribs.

"Hi. Sorry about that," I said. "It's just, you know, you look like—"

The glare that was shot at me shut me up. Shane nodded gravely to El before glowering at me as he spoke. "I don't have time for this. Charlie's gone missing again. I was just about to go looking for him."

"You need to keep your windows closed," El said. At my confused look, she added, "Charlie's Shane's cat."

"Oh." I paused and then realized a way I could make it up to them. "Hey. I can help. If you've got some fur, I could probably locate him for you."

El hastily added, "He's a new wizard."

"M… wizard." I nodded and surreptitiously rubbed my ribs. Damn, the pixie had sharp elbows.

"A new wizard," Shane said guardedly before he shut the door in our faces.

The pair of us traded looks while, within, we could hear loud movement. Just as I was about to knock again, the door flew open and Shane held his hand out. The hairball he dropped into my hand made me wrinkle my nose in disgust.

"This work?"

"Should…" I called upon the knowledge of the Link spell. A few hand gestures later, the hairball glowed, a line of red appearing before my eyes.

Link Cast
Synchronicity 63%

"Well?" Shane said, and I blinked.

"This way." I turned to take the staircase down. The line led diagonally downward, showing the shortest route from me to the cat, I presumed. Which of course didn't take into account minor things like floors, walls, and gravity. As I walked, tendrils of red would flash for a second from the hairball before dying. Each new tendril, each second that I held the original connection, drained my mana as I focused on keeping the spell tuned to Charlie.

We walked down the stairs and around the corner, though an alleyway, and out a side street to another alleyway. I barely paid attention to my surroundings other than ensuring there were no metallic death machines barreling down the road when I crossed. By the time we made it across the street, a slow-growing headache had begun to form as my mana depleted at an astonishing rate. Just as I was about to release the spell, I heard a cry of happiness behind me.

"Charlie! There you are, you horrid beast!" Shane shoved me aside as he ran forward. Charlie, rather than a feisty tomcat with a patch for an eye, was instead an elegant Persian who proceeded to snuggle into Shane's beard, almost disappearing in the dwarf's arms. "Thank you. Charlie always does this, but ever since those damn weres moved in down the street, I don't dare let him run around outside. Never know when they'd get hungry!"

"Do werewolves eat cats?" I asked, and Shane looked me straight in the eye and nodded.

"Aye. And don't let them tell you otherwise! Why, Mrs. Brindle down my hall lost her Angie just a week after those weres moved in."

El made a face as Shane continued to speak, one that was lost to him as he snuggled his cat. "Well, we should get a move on. I need to show Henry around a bit more."

"Of course, of course. I should get Charlie back in." As Shane neared me, he looked up and said, "There a way to contact you, Wizard? If I need Charlie found again, I mean."

"You can call me for now," El interjected before I could say anything. Shane just nodded, accepting this piece of knowledge with equanimity. Only when he was gone did I turn to El and raise an eyebrow. "You're not ready to let them know where you live," she explained. "For one thing, you need some wards on your home."

"Haven't learned that yet," I said, and El snorted.

"I would hope not. It takes years for an enchanter to gain sufficient knowledge to ward a building properly. Now, come on. Let's get this over with."

I followed along after the diminutive pixie, a half smile on my face as I contemplated the dwarf and his cat. It might not have been much, but using my magic for something other than killing rats or practice had actually made me feel good. Useful.

***

"El, why are we doing this?" I asked the pixie hours later. We were splitting a bowl of nachos for supper.

"Because I'm hungry," said El as she waved a nacho laden with jalapenos and cheese.

"No, not supper. The meet and greet." I nodded my head toward where our server, a long, thin praying mantis-like humanoid, took orders from a pair of frat boys. I had to smile internally as they goaded one another to hit on their server when she left. Unfocusing my eyes a little, I could understand why—the tall, leggy blonde glamour was quite the looker.

"Safety," El said and waved her hand around. "We need to get you introduced and your story straight. Until you learn to control your aura, you're glowing like a Christmas tree with all the arcane energy you're giving off. Anyone with the sight—or who has an enchantment to let them *see*, which is most everyone—can tell you're a new… wizard."

"Oh." I sat back and thought about it. If she was right and I did look like a floodlight, then there wasn't a way for me to hide my magic. Since I wasn't apprenticed, I couldn't be introduced as a mage, so I had to be a wizard, a new one at that— which set up my story and let others dismiss me. "Thanks."

"*De nada.*" El waved my thanks away.

"Why are you helping me, El?" I asked. "After the first time—"

"Oh, Henry," El said quietly. "I didn't want you to be part of this world. But since you seem bent on joining us, I might as well make sure you survive it. At least for a little while."

The last few words were said softly, so softly I didn't think El meant for me to hear them. I still didn't understand her wariness, and Lily's. So far, everyone we'd met had been nice and civil. Well, other than the orcs, but muggers were muggers. You didn't expect them to be nice. Still… "Thank you."

El flashed me a smile before she turned back to her beer and nachos.

Chapter 8

The next couple of weeks were filled with small, minor quests that were generated by the supernatural denizens of my neighborhood. Once El had finished introducing me around that evening, I'd become just another fixture, their very own wizard. What no one had told me was that wizards were relatively rare and occasionally useful to know. However, few magic users were approachable, often being the supernatural equivalent of shut-ins. After all, unlike me, most magic users had to spend hours memorizing and then practicing spells over and over again. Spending time running minor errands was the last thing on their minds.

The quests offered to me never ranged into "Fetch ten silver-capped mushrooms from the Forest of Never-Ending Anguish," but were more along the lines of "My walk-in freezer broke down. Could you chill my meat until the repairman gets here?" or "Can you please babysit my brood of a half dozen hyperactive ratkin?" By the way, if anyone ever asks you about that last one, the answer is "hell no." There's a reason Mrs. Umber had to ask an unemployed, newly developed wizard.

Unlike my rat quest, these minor quests—or errands, if you will—did not provide much in terms of experience gain. Spending an evening learning how to adjust my Light spell to cast different colored lights for a vampire-only soiree might not have been particularly exciting, once you got over the fact the vampires had no desire to drink your blood, but it was educational. And, if I did so say so myself, quite beautiful. Interesting fact—vampires were allergic to sunlight due to a specific curse by a sun god. It meant that light, even one filled with ultraviolet light, did nothing to vampires. It was why most vampires actually had a decent tan, even in winter. What better way to throw off hunters than not looking like a pale, gangly monster?

Unfortunately, Mend turned out to be significantly less useful than first envisioned. The spell actually encouraged previously separated pieces together, mending fractures and rips. It was, in some ways, very similar to the Heal spell. However, it also required a degree of finesse to work properly. A Mend spell on a broken button would fix the edges of the strings but might do so with the button on the outside. In that, like so many other things, magic was less useful than a little hard work with needle and thread. After weeks of working with magic, much of my initial excitement had worn away with the realization that magic was cool, but more often than not, mundane solutions won out. It was disappointing but at least partly explained why mages didn't rule the world; magic was useful, but so was plain old science.

All in all, the next few weeks saw a slow but gradual increase in strength and ability as I pushed my own knowledge of magic. Whether it was learning to hit and maintain a specific temperature with my spells, altering the color of light, or avoiding concussions while babysitting—those kids were vicious—I had managed to actually gain another level.

Class: Mage
Level 4 (12% Experience)
Known Spells: Light Sphere, Force Missile, Heat, Freeze, Chime, Breeze, Lesser Shield, Heal, Link, Mend, Ward

Unlike my previous level gain, there were fewer changes in my spells. I might have gotten better at controlling the spells themselves, but according to Lily, the major changes required me to improve significantly more.

Ward, on the other hand, was my first warding spell. It actually wasn't a complete spell by itself; each Ward spell had to be combined with another spell before it could be activated, and it required me to physically carve the ward into an object. A Light Ward, for example, basically created a fixed light spell that could, with a small exertion of will, be turned on or off. At least until the spell charge died.

At my current level, all I could do was put up wards that could be triggered by simple events— an exertion of magical will, the opening or closing of a door, physical pressure. I could not even chain more than one spell together at a time, a prerequisite for actual, workable wards. Still, it didn't stop me from spending half a day carving wards onto various pieces of furniture throughout the house. I only stopped when Lily promised to turn me into a lump of salt if I didn't stop.

Over the course of the few weeks, perhaps the greatest gain I saw was in the understanding of the information Lily had downloaded into my mind. I began to understand mana and magic, and how mana was just a short-form placeholder for the power of creation itself. Mages were people who were able to manipulate mana, using incantations and spell formulas to do what they desired. In truth, after speaking with Lily and El a bit, mages weren't even the most powerful or competent group. Clerics, shamans, and other faith workers could all manipulate mana just as well, though they were often restricted by the tenets of their faiths and their gods.

Furthermore, the incantations and spell formulas didn't matter. It was why there were so many branches of magic to study in the world. It was not the words themselves, but the intentions and mental energy expended that dictated the formation of the spells. By focusing the mind and that "mana muscle" that mages had, they could cast spells, channeling them through their body as appropriate to their gift. Rumors were that the most powerful mages could cast spells with just a thought. Of course, I was miles away from anything like that.

All things said and done, the last few weeks had been peaceful and surprisingly fulfilling. Running deliveries for El when I had no other quests to do, helping out in the neighborhood and receiving pay for it all, it was fun. For once in my life, I actually thought I was getting somewhere.

I should have known it would never last.

***

The first sign of trouble was the shattered basement door. The second was the raised voices as Lily argued with a stranger in our home. I formed a Force Missile in my hand, holding it low so it couldn't be seen easily, and stepped across my threshold to meet the danger. After all, that was what heroes did.

Lily was standing in front of her computer, hands on her hips and one foot tapping the ground, as she argued with my intruder. My intruder, who towered over the diminutive genie, was clad in grey slacks, a cream button-down shirt, and a long, black woolen coat. He could easily have walked around downtown and not drawn a glance, which made his presence in my rundown basement apartment even stranger.

"…you will come with me!" the stranger finished demanding when I stepped in. Like a trigger, he swiveled around to glare at me before his gaze fixed on my ring. Without even speaking, he raised his hand, fingers splaying around and twisting a few times before he jerked it toward himself. For the briefest of moments, I felt a tugging on the ring before I clenched my fist tight, and the tugging faded.

Out-of-level opponent encountered.
Please increase level before continuing encounter.

Unknown Assailant (Mage Level 187)

"No. You can't take his ring away," Lily said, snapping at the man. "I told you. It's useless."

"What in the blazes?" the man growled and raised his hand, repeating what had to be a spell. This time, there wasn't even a faint tug.

"Stop that!" I snapped at him and added, "And who the hell are you?"

"How—?" Eyes narrowed, the man stared at me and my hand while he ignored my question. With a shrug, he strode over to me and grabbed at my hand, coming to a stop inches away from my body. Reflexively, I swung the hand that held the Force Missile and watched the formed spell shatter a foot away from the man's body, a rainbow of colors rippling from the point of impact.

"A wizard," the man snarled, and he flicked a finger and pointed it at me. A Force Spear formed and shot toward my face faster than I could react. Before it reached me, the Force Spear disappeared as if it had never existed.

"What?" we both cried out in unison.

Out-of-level opponent encountered.

Please increase level before continuing encounter.

Again, the words flashed in front of my face, and this time, I actually read them. Out of level? Oh! Like the orcs.

"Genie! You did this." The man turned and snarled at Lily who smirked at him.

"Yes, I did. Told you, you aren't taking his ring," Lily said once more.

"Who are you?" I demanded again, glaring at the man as I moved away from him, courage bolstered by the fact that he really couldn't do anything. It seemed whatever Lily had done, it worked both ways and stopped me from hurting him too.

"I am Caleb Hahn, Magus of the Third Circle, and I demand you return that ring," Caleb said, drawing himself to his full height.

If he thought to intimidate me by looming, he'd chosen the wrong person. I'd grown up my whole life as the short Asian, and after a while, you either learned to ignore the height disparity or just became totally screwed over by it. I glared right back at him, my hand clenched tight as I snapped. "No. Now fuck off before I call the cops."

"The cops! You would call mundane humans on this, you unworthy peasant?" Caleb said.

"Well, yeah. You broke my door, and you are refusing to leave. I can't hurt you, and you can't hurt me." I pulled out my cell phone. "Now, you leaving or not?"

Caleb's eyes grew wide, and he spluttered a few more times, something about the sanctity of supernatural affairs, but his clarity was not helped by Lily giggling and holding her sides next to me. When I started dialing, Caleb finally threw his hands up and stalked out of the room, retreating with as much dignity as he could.

Asshole never even offered to fix my door either. Thankfully, with a little elbow grease and the Mend spell, the door was an easy patch since he had only busted the knob itself. It was after all that was done with that I had time to speak with Lily.

"So, what was that about?" I asked Lily, who was looking uncharacteristically serious when I turned to look at her.

"That was meant to be the end of this," Lily replied, waving her hand around. "But now that we've thwarted them—I love that word, thwarted—they'll have to regroup and think about it."

"I know what it was. I want to know what it *was* about," I said.

"Ah." Lily paused, staring at me before answering. "The ring. It was previously owned by a mage in the order. You probably realized that. They wanted the ring and me back."

"Finders keepers not a thing in the supernatural world?" I asked lightly.

"No," Lily said bitingly, glaring at me till she realized I was taking this seriously. "They will be back."

"Can they break the wish? Or am I going to be expecting a lot of, ummm… how many circles are there?"

"Seven. But they'd have to send an apprentice to deal with you," Lily said. "You wouldn't even qualify for one of their circles yet."

"But, I'm level four!" I spluttered.

"Uh huh, and the minimum level to get out of being an apprentice would be around level twenty or so, I'd say. And to actually become a member of the council, you'd have to be level forty at least. Maybe fifty," Lily said.

"Oh…" I frowned. "But my spells—"

"Are a cheat. You can cast certain spells because of what I've given you, but your understanding of magic itself is pitiful."

"Hey!"

"Could you recreate any of your spells yourself?" Lily shot back.

"Umm…" I frowned, thinking about it. I focused for a second, trying to recreate the Light spell from basics. After all, it was the spell I used the most and thus should have been most familiar with. The beginning was simple. I could remember that part easily enough. About a third of the way in, I realized I was having to cudgel my brain to extract the necessary mental gymnastics required to continue casting the spell. About halfway through, I felt the spell fizzle, the feedback sending a spike of pain through my head like an icepick through my eye. "Aaarggh."

"Told you," Lily said.

I grunted, rubbing at my eyes as the pain faded. Fine. Perhaps I relied on the ready-made, intuitive spells she had provided too much.

"It'll be a while before they actually send someone though. The council isn't very quick at making decisions or changing their minds." Lily fixed me with a glare. "However, that doesn't mean you can slack off. Once they decide to move, they will move."

"Yeah, but if I get better, my level goes up and they can throw more at me."

"You do realize that 'levels' aren't exactly accurate? I mean, it's one thing to stop a Third-Circle Mage coming at you, but if they aren't putting out magic like a sun, things start getting a bit more complicated. A mugger or a hitman, from my perspective, is only a few levels difference but from yours is significant," Lily said, and I grunted.

She had a point. And rather more importantly, I hadn't chosen to learn magic so I could hide in a corner at the first sign of trouble. If I was going to learn magic, I was going to learn it properly. Which meant… "I'm going to need better quests then."

As Lily smiled, I felt a chill go through my body.

Chapter 9

Five feet tall, red, muscular, and naked with a pair of horns, a whiplike tail, and tiny wings that couldn't support a bat, the imp raised his fist, ready pound me into the floor again in the back kitchen of the Italian mom-and-pop shop we were battling in. Thankfully, the imp was a lot like my high school bullies, all strength, no finesse, and the haymaker he threw was telegraphed from a mile away.

I ducked underneath the punch, losing a precious second as I wobbled on my feet, my balance still a bit shot from earlier blows. I twisted my fingers in a circle and pointed as I chanted the words "Force Missile." A ball of blue and green formed in the circle, shooting forward as I finished chanting and pointing, striking the imp in its chest.

Force Missile Cast
89% Synchronicity

Force Bolt does 15 damage to Lesser Imp.

The attack just pissed the imp off further, and it swung a tight uppercut that caught me in the chest, throwing my frail form backward. I smashed into the closed refrigerator door and groaned, the back of my head sending pain signals from where it had been knocked around even further.

Henry Alfred Chan Hock Tsien dealt 23 damage by Lesser Imp.

Even as I twisted my fingers around to cast another spell, the imp battered my hand away disdainfully. Through tear-filled eyes, I stared at my would-be murderer.

Lesser Imp (Level 4)
HP: 13/43

Before the monster could finish me off, a thrown cast-iron pan caught it on the back of its head. I swore I saw a little red -1 float off the top of its head, though I wasn't sure if that was just the incipient concussion or an actual artifact of Lily tinkering with the wish. The imp, distracted, turned around and stalked to its new prey.

"Do something!" Chantelle Rossi, the imp's attacker and my current quest-giver, screamed at me as she scrambled around the kitchen for more things to throw at the monster.

Reminded I wasn't part of the audience in this life-or-death struggle, I cast my Force Missile spell. Once again, I received a notification with an 84 percent synchronicity rate, more than enough to deal the damage needed to end the imp. This time, when the Force Missile hit, it cracked the monster's skull, leaving its corpse slumped against the sink. I groaned, sitting down as I stared at the blinking blue bar that indicated I had nearly no mana left.

Lesser Imp (Level 4) Defeated!

My benefactor was not taking the sudden change in fortunes in stride, instead having scooped up a pan to smash the dead monster around a few more times. Only when it did not attempt to defend itself did she stop. Chantelle stood over the dead monster, long, black hair disheveled and white blouse popped open, green blood staining it. When she turned to me, eyes sparkling with fury, her lips pulled into a snarl.

"You! You were hired to fix the problem, not make it worse," she snapped as she stalked toward me, waving the bloody pot in her hand. A piece of pasta, resiliently holding on against the tyranny of gravity, finally succumbed and dropped to the ground, landing by her feet. This, thankfully, made her pause in her tirade long enough for me to get a word in.

"Sorry! I… it was just supposed to be a level-four imp!" I spluttered as I pushed myself up, my chest aching as I breathed. Damn demon had fists like boulders.

"What do you mean 'level four'?" the raven-haired proprietress said, shaking her head. "Look at this mess. You're going to cost us more to have the place fixed up than the damage the imp was doing!"

At Chantelle's accusation, I slowly—very slowly as my neck and head were still throbbing—surveyed the room. Shattered glassware, spilled food, a few broken cupboards, and a hole in the microwave from an errant Force Missile greeted my eyes in quick succession.

"Sorry… I'll, ummm…"

"We're taking the imp's body. And don't expect to get paid!"

"But… I—"

A quick shake of the pot was enough to make me back down. A few more apologies and I finally managed to extricate myself from the kitchen and Rossi's, her family restaurant, without being beaten to death. Outside, I paused for a second to take in the beautiful, clear day and breathed in the clear, clean air. On the opposite side of the street, a few others stared at me strangely, basking in the sunlight, including a bespectacled teenager who was actually glaring. I had to smile as I relaxed and shook off the berating I had received. I was alive and learning magic. What else could I ask for?

***

As I got out of my Ryde and tapped my phone to acknowledge having been dropped off, I found myself grateful I'd decided to skip biking. My head throbbed, my back spasmed, and I found myself fumbling my keys to my basement suite. I kicked the door closed behind me, whimpered at the loud noise, and crashed on my futon.

When I woke up later that evening, almost all my injuries were healed once again. A quick perusal of the notifications explained things to me.

Henry Alfred Chan Hock Tsien is well rested. +5% Experience Gain for 4 hours.
Henry Alfred Chan Hock Tsien has gained 37 health points due to resting.

Huh. I really needed to get Lily to stop messing with the notifications, but ever since she'd seen a bill with my full name, she'd been on this kick of putting it everywhere. As my stomach growled, I got up to throw a ready-made pizza in the oven. I turned my head to stare at the jinn who was hovering over my computer. I had thought picking up a second laptop for myself would have freed up a computer for my use. Instead, Lily had just decided to take them both over and was running two different games at the same time.

"That was not a level-four imp," I grumped at Lily. Silence lingered for so long I thought she might not have heard me, punctuated only by the tapping on the keyboard and click of her mouse.

"Yes, it was," Lily said. "You just suck at fighting."

"I'm supposed to be good at it?" I muttered, shaking my head. The imp had been my second combat quest, and I had to admit, she was right. At least I hadn't gotten bitten, but it wasn't as if I'd ever had any real experience fighting for my life.

Scraps with schoolyard bullies and the occasional mugging did not count after all. I wasn't a soldier or police officer or a martial artist. I was just a guy who liked computer and role-playing games and had found a magic ring.

"You ready for the next one?" Lily asked. "Goddamn noob, do your job…"

"Ummm…" I glared at Lily, but since she wasn't bothering to look up, the glare did just about nothing. In the end, I gave up. "You know, I'm new at this, but calling me a noob is a little rude."

"Not you. It's this damn cleric. Can't heal for shit. I'm dying here," Lily said, a hand briefly waving at her game. She turned her head to the side, eyeing the other game before returning to the one she was focused on. It seemed in the second game, she was flying some spaceship that was moving on autopilot, stars shifting as she kept turning and jumping. "Though, if the shoe fits…"

"Whatever," I growled. "You said you have a new quest?"

"Take your pick," Lily said, pointing to a pile of papers. I frowned, walking to them, picking them up, and scanning the headlines.

Persistent Slime Mold is Eating Away My Floors. Clean It Out! $200

Leprechaun Escapee. Capture and Return. No Corpses! 185 Gold Coins and a Brindell Tulip

Become a Hellhound Trainer! No Special Skills Required. We Will Train on the Job! Fair Compensation.

The Grey Angels Hospice is Looking for Healers! Volunteer Your Time with Our Great Staff and Residents.

Required — an Experienced Exorcist! $350

Gremlin Squatter Removal. $500

I stared at the printouts, a sneaking suspicion confirmed when I looked at the web address printed on the top. "Is this a classifieds website?"

"Mmmhmmm… hey! Give that back," Lily shouted a moment later as I pulled my new laptop onto my lap.

"Hush." I tabbed away from her game. Within seconds, I was at the site. Or what would have been the site if not for a big "Password Protected" sign. A couple seconds of fumbling indicated Lily had not saved her password either. "How do I get in?"

"You don't," Lily said, tapping furiously at her keyboard for a few seconds before turning to me. "That's way too much responsibility for you right now."

"Oh, come on. I'm just going to browse it."

"Too dangerous."

"Browsing?" I said. "I promise not to download any viruses."

"And how about spells, demonic entities, and mana taps?"

"Uhhh…" I paused, pushing the laptop away from me slightly. "Demons can come through the web?" That just sounded like a bad B-movie setup.

"Not normally, but that website isn't on the normal Internet. It's a separate dimensional nexus that the supernatural use, and the defenses that have been applied against such incursions are relaxed there. Otherwise, only entities on this dimension could post on it," Lily said.

At her words, I edged even farther away from my laptop, my eyes wide. "There are other-dimensional beings posting on that!? Like gods and demons and Lovecraft monsters?"

"And angels. Jinn. Fae. Dragons. Ice giants," Lily continued on. "Of course there are. Merl's Web is the most popular communication form right now. Not that there aren't competing sites, but Merl seems to have kept up with the times."

"Merl… Merlin?" I asked suspiciously.

"Yes. The old codger might be trapped, but he's still got his hand in the pie." Lily shook her head. "Once I got back in touch with him, he pointed me to the site."

"Merlin's alive." I sat with a thump, staring at Lily. You'd think that after months of all this, I would have gotten used to being surprised. But still… "And Arthur?"

"Dead. Or sleeping. Don't know. You'd have to ask Merl. Not that he's talking." Lily shrugged her shoulders. "He's, you know, a bit annoyed about all that."

"How about Lancelot? Gawain? The Green Knight? The Holy Grail?"

"Ques-ting," Lily drawled and pointed to the papers again.

I growled softly, but even repeated prodding had her repeating the same word again and again. Eventually, I gave up and went over the quests available. A good half of them seemed to involve killing, finding, or eradicating something. There were no "fetch" quests, probably because I received more than enough of those from El, who at least knew enough to give me exact directions. It wasn't as if I knew where to find fairy dust or three-eyed spotted mushrooms. In the end, I highlighted a couple I was willing to do and handed them to Lily.

"Right. Out then. Once I get details, you'll know."

"That's it?" I frowned, having expected, well, more details now.

"Yes. Now shoo. We're running the Virtuous Grotto, and I don't need you bothering me," Lily said, waving me away.

Kicked out of my apartment, I grabbed my jacket on the way out. Ah well, maybe El had something interesting.

***

After making my way to Nora's, I found El seated at the counter, smiling cheerfully at an unexpected mundane customer. I watched El for a second, my gaze unfocused to see her as her glamour rather than her true form before refocusing my eyes. I had to admire the svelte figure she cut, at least underneath her glamour. Though I had to wonder, what did it look like if someone saw me checking her out and was unable to see through her glamor? On the other hand, one could never tell with others' tastes.

"Henry?" Her voice brought me out of my ruminations, and I realized her customer had left. "Did you need something?"

"No." I shook my head. Then, girding up my courage, I stepped up to the counter, flashing her a smile. "Actually—"

"No."

"You didn't even—"

"Henry, I'm four hundred and thirty-six years old. I know what you were going to ask. And the answer is no," El said and smiled at me gently.

"Well, ummmm…" I paused, staring at El. I felt slightly deflated at having my advances shot down even before I'd gotten started. I looked around, awkward now, as I kicked myself for even trying. I should have known better. After all, El had never indicated any interest in me before beyond a general kindly interest in my well-being.

Pretty much what you'd expect a big sister to show a little brother in fact.

"It's not personal, Henry. I might only be a lesser fae, but I am fae. I'll live for thousands of years, and well, as a human mage…" El said, shrugging her shoulders. "It's better this way."

"Oh…" I nodded slightly. I guess that made sense. I mean, the elves in the *Lord of the Rings* series were like that too. And I was no Aragorn.

"So, is there anything else you came in for?"

"Not really. I actually thought you might have something for me to do," I answered, looking back up to see El smiling at me patiently.

"Mmmm… not sure I need to remodel the shop yet."

I winced. "You heard about that."

"Just a little. Showing you around kind of tied you to me," El said.

"Yeah, sorry about that. The imp was tougher than I thought," I said, shrugging my shoulders.

"It's fine. Used to be you couldn't swing a cat without hitting a magical troubleshooter. Now, everyone wants to be an office mage or animator or enchanter," El said, shaking her head. "I guess it works out for you though—otherwise no one would hire you."

"Thanks?" I shook my head again. "Anyway, did you have anything you need me to help with?"

"Actually," El said, smiling slightly and reaching under the counter. In her hand when she lifted it was a simple, brown-paper-wrapped package.

I took it automatically, jiggling it slightly and noting a clink of glass containers before I slid it into my black messenger bag.

"Don't do that! What if it was salamander spit?"

"Ummm…"

"It's highly explosive." El sighed.

"So, is it?"

"No. And you shouldn't be asking what's in the packages. You know that," El said exasperatedly, shaking her head. "It's arthritis rub for Grandma Gail." A quick scribble and she handed me the address on a Post-it note.

"I thought I wasn't supposed to know what was in there," I said.

"You're not normally, but you're going to need to know for this. Now, be polite and nice. You're going into orc territory." El held a finger up. "Just tell them what and who you're delivering for, and they'll leave you alone. Got it?"

"You sell to orcs?" I asked incredulously.

"I sell *arthritis medicine* to everyone," El said. "What, you think I should let Grandma Gail suffer because she's green and tusky?"

"No…" I said, stepping back at the heat in El's voice.

"Get it through your head, Henry. This isn't your fantasy books. These are people with their own hopes and dreams and lives. We're just people trying to get by in a world that isn't necessarily set up for us."

"Sorry. I'm sorry. I'll do better," I said. At El's nod, I backed out and headed off to do her little courier job. Head hunched, I pulled out my phone and punched in the address to work out the fastest way to do this. One day, I'd get a car, but that would have to wait till I had a more regular and consistent source of income, one that did not rely on charity and magical windfalls.

***

Faircreek in the southwestern part of the city once hosted the city's docks. In the 1960s, the city had rebuilt the docks farther downriver, outside of the city proper, to handle the additional business. Now, Faircreek was a mixture of rundown warehouses, squat concrete buildings, and crumbling docks along with a few over-burdened homeless shelters. Dotted throughout the neighborhood were failed attempts at revitalization, the scenic concrete-and-grass walkways along the river unkept and not cleaned, a pair of soaring condos looming over their older cousins. It was no place to go if you weren't a resident, the natural resting place for those who had nowhere else to go.

Not surprisingly, even though I'd lived in the city my whole life, I'd only been down this way twice—once entirely by accident, the second on an ill-advised attempt at a hip-hop concert to impress a date. As I sat on the worn-down upholstery of the bus, waiting for my stop, I stared at the residents with new eyes, El's words still ringing in my mind.

Hunched over, hooded figures slunk from corner to corner, hands in baggy clothing. Under hoods, I caught glimpses of inhuman features—snouts, whiskers, fur, and more. Many had the barest of glamours on, just enough to pass a cursory inspection. Interestingly enough, most glamours showed the individuals as minorities. Perhaps most surprisingly was their number, one in seven, one in eight of those on the streets were inhuman—a higher percentage by far than anywhere else.

We're just people trying to get by in a world that isn't necessarily set up for us.

How hard was life for a supernatural if your funds had to go to not only food but glamour as well? If you had to cover up, hide your identity to survive? If the assholes who were casting glamour spells decided it cost "extra" to make you not look like a minority? I'd stumbled across magic and lucked out finding the golden ring, taking power by choice. Many of those I saw on the streets, they'd never had a choice.

They were somber thoughts to think as I got off the bus and glanced at my phone one last time.

I walked the streets to my destination, idly noting I was a good six blocks away.

As I walked, I tried to remember all the hints about safely traversing a bad neighborhood I had ever read. Walk with purpose and keep looking around, but don't make eye contact for too long. Avoid touching, but don't act scared. You'd think that wielding magic would have made this walk easier, but now that I could see the scales, furs, and tusks of the denizens of this city, it really didn't. It didn't help that I probably shone like a beacon to everyone else too.

I was two-thirds of the way to my destination before I encountered my first problem. A group of orcs, hanging out on the corner in hoodies, torn jeans, and leather gloves, stared at me as I neared them. The stares intensified even as I stepped to the side in an attempt to go around the group, an attempt that was foiled by a large, blocky body.

"What you doing here, Wizard?" The blocker stood in front of me, glaring down at my form.

"Uh…" I blinked and gulped, stepping back. That was a mistake as the orc stepped forward immediately, continuing to crowd me.

"Well? This ain't your neighborhood."

I opened my mouth to say something, but my throat closed with fear. While a part of me knew I was probably—probably—fine due to Lily's wish, all my lizard brain knew was that there were a half dozen large, green, and very muscular figures looking at me aggressively. A pair of hands came up and shoved me backward, sending me stumbling back into a figure I hadn't even realized was behind me.

"You going to say something, boy?"

"Delivery," I croaked out and then cleared my throat, trying again as I pulled myself straight. "Delivery for El. From El. For Grandma… ummmm…" Shit. My mind blanked on her name, the rush of adrenaline making my hands clammy. The looming figures and the casual bump against my shoulder as they crowded me made my breath tighten.

"Grandma…?" One of the orcs snorted before another smacked him on the arm with the back of his hand.

"You delivering the medicine for Grandma Gail?" the smackee asked, and I nodded in dumb relief. "Should have said so." A quick set of hand waves had the orcs stepping back, giving me breathing room. Without even waiting for me to recover, the speaker had already started walking. "Sorry about that. El never told us she was using a wizard for delivery."

"It's fine. I'm new," I muttered, relief washing through my body as we walked toward our destination.

"Oh, shit," the orc muttered just before the loud blare of a siren went off behind us.

Cruising to a stop, a police car stopped us half a block from the apartment building I was to make the delivery at. Inwardly, I cursed, getting nervous once more. It was strange how I could get nervous even if I was doing nothing wrong in the presence of police.

From out of the police car came an elf, a damn elf with pointed ears, long hair, gleaming teeth, and a smirk. A human, who glowed just like me, came to stand beside me. I frowned, staring at the pair, and after a moment, their information finally populated.

Police Elf (Level 28)

Police Mage (Level 32)

"What do we have here?" the elf said, smirking at us as he walked toward us. The orc was standing beside me, hands held to the side and away from his body, his face fixed. "A wizard and an orc walking down the street."

"Uhhh…" I said and then decided to clamp my mouth shut. Surprising fact about having conversations about the supernatural in public— no one cared. Between fantasy movies, LARPers and just normal human self-conceit, the occasional overheard conversation was easily dismissed. Still, most supernaturals weren't this blatant. Then again, this wasn't exactly your normal suburban neighborhood either.

"Witch got your tongue, Wizard?" the elf said, staring at me, baton suddenly in his hand. He moved so smoothly and quickly I didn't see it again until it was under my chin and pushing my head up. A hot flash of anger went through me, but I forced it down.

"Just doing a delivery," I said hoarsely, fighting the roiling emotions of anger, shame, and fear running through me. Damn it.

A hand went to my bag, and I automatically moved to push it aside. A second later, I found myself on the ground, a knee ground into the small of my back, one hand outstretched and the other curled around my body, pain radiating from my knee and chin where I had been slammed into the ground when the human had tossed me down.

"Trying to stop us from doing our job, are you?" A crank on my arm made me grunt in pain. The strap of my bag was pulled aside, and I felt the tension suddenly release, the bag pulled out from underneath me not too gently.

"I wasn't—"

"Lying to a police officer. Tsk..." the mage said, shaking his head. "I hate your kind. Thinking you're all something because you learned a little magic."

"I—"

"Shut up," the orc growled at me and then released a sudden exhalation of breath shortly after a meaty *thunk*.

I couldn't turn my head, and any attempt at moving resulted in another shooting pain from my arm.

"Andy, Andy, Andy, I thought you knew better," the elf said mockingly. I heard the clasp of my bag open and then the noise of the contents of my bag hitting the ground. The muffled *thunk* of the package, my notebook, and the rest of the random crap that I kept in my bag reached my ears. A short while later, I heard the tearing of paper before a dull *thunk* of glass on concrete. I found myself exhaling in thanks that all of El's packages were in ultra-tough, enchanted containers. "What is this? Hmmm…?"

A sharp jab in my back made me arch slightly.

"We're talking to you, Wizard," the mage said.

"Arthritis remedy," I said through stolen breaths.

"Really?" Indistinct noises and a loud sniff later, an open bottle landed on the ground next to me along with its lid and the remaining bottles. "Smells like shit. You peddling shit, Wizard?"

"I'm just bringing it for El," I said.

"El, El, El… that little troublesome pixie," the elf muttered. "I thought she knew better than to deal with scum like this. Well, I guess we'll just have to do something about that."

"What?" I asked as I twisted my head around. The mage let me do so briefly before he reapplied pressure, forcing me to look on futilely as the elf raised his booted foot and came down on the bottle. It shattered under his boot, his foot rising again. Anger flashed through me, at the mage and the elf and the damn orc who just stood there…

The elf raised his foot again to smash another bottle. "Now, be sure to tell El—"

"That's enough, Quinn," a low, husky, and dangerous voice said from the opposite side of my head. "You've had your fun."

"Marc," the elf said, sudden wariness in his voice. I could feel the mage above me shift his weight, turning toward the newcomer.

"Let him go," the same voice growled, and my arm was released. Footsteps shifted, and as I sat up slowly, rubbing my shoulder, I noted the policemen had backed off, staring at the newcomer. I turned my head to look as well and had to agree—the newcomer was definitely worth staring at. Where Andy, my erstwhile guide, had been big, the newcomer could have fronted for an NFL team at nearly seven feet tall and nearly half again as broad. Behind the newcomer was another trio of orcs, none as large as he was but only by a hairbreadth.

"Just making sure the wizard knows what's what," the elf said, smirking still. However, I noticed the pair had their hands near their guns now and were, in fact, moving back to their car easily. "No harm done."

Under the watchful eyes of the orcs, the pair of policeman left. I pulled together my bag, stuffed everything together, and held the broken straps in hand while my emotions raged. I could Mend them, but unlike some, I preferred to keep my magic to quieter and less public locations.

"Well, boy? You going to make your delivery?" the orc snapped at me, and I blinked, nodding quickly. I moved forward, hesitating for a second when he held a hand up to Andy to stop him from coming with me. A quick look told me his signal wasn't for me, and so I headed up the stairs.

You'd think after all that, that Grandma Gail was some mythical, powerful shaman or the power behind the throne. Instead, Grandma Gail was exactly what you'd have expected of a grandmother—old, bent, wrinkled, and in this case, green. She was more than grateful for the delivery and completely forgiving about the single broken bottle. Two hours later, filled with tea and cookies, I tottered out of the grateful orc's neat apartment, surprised to see Andy waiting for me.

"Andy?"

"I'll walk you back," Andy said and then held his hand out.

Taking the dollar bills from him automatically, I frowned as I stared at them.

"For El. For the broken bottle."

"Uhh…" I paused, unsure.

"Just take it. I should have seen them coming," Andy said, and I nodded dumbly as I fell into step with him.

"They do that often?" I asked.

"Every chance they get. Fucking pigs like to hassle us," Andy said, shaking his head. "They pick on us in particular because, well, you know."

Because they were orcs. "Sorry."

"Why are you sorry?" Andy growled at me, and I winced, ducking my head. After a moment, Andy shook his head. "Never mind. It's not your fault."

"Yeah. Assholes," I grumbled, running my finger over the mended strap. Even now, I could feel the slight raises and bumpiness from the Mend spell. At least I was getting better with the spell. Still, a part of me twisted at how easily I'd rolled over. But what was I supposed to do? They were cops. And higher levels than me. In sullen silence, the pair of us made our way back to the bus stop where we stood, brooding over our respective failures. The bus, when it arrived, found us still standing in silence.

"Take care, Wizard. Try not to get beaten up by cops again, eh?" Andy said, waving goodbye as I got on.

I had to chuckle slightly, nodding back to Andy. Well, that had been enlightening and humbling, if somewhat less than useful for my leveling. Then again, perhaps not all experience needed to come with levels.

***

Hours later, I was back home. Lily, surprisingly, was not on the computer but standing over the oven. I eyed the dark-haired genie as she stirred a pot of instant noodles and then walked to my computers without a word. On them, blue screens showed the software had updated. That was one mystery easily solved.

"Lily," I said, walking over to lean against a cupboard. "Wanted to ask you about something."

"Sure," Lily said, eyes raking over me.

I quickly explained my encounter with the orcs and the cops, finishing with: "How come the cops were able to touch me? I mean, they were obviously out of level."

"Thought it might be that," Lily said, tapping her spoon against the pot before she carefully poured the contents into a waiting bowl. "The answer is that the encounter was a social challenge, not a physical one."

"Felt pretty physical to me," I grumbled, rubbing my still-sore shoulder.

"Only because you failed your social check," Lily said, looking up at me.

"I don't really get that you know," I said. "I mean, what makes it a social encounter rather than a physical one? Aren't most encounters social till, well, they're not?"

"Mmmm… yes." Lily paused and then waved a hand to the computers before she returned to stirring the bowl. "But we're talking about your wish and the way I set it up. And I did it by watching the games. If you run into a city and start ganking the guards, you don't expect to get away with it, do you? Same thing here. The police, most legal authorities, are going to be exempt."

"But those guys were assholes," I said, grumbling. "It'd have been nice if they couldn't have grabbed me."

"And then what?" Lily said, raising an eyebrow. "Do you think the fact that they couldn't touch you would deescalate the situation? Make them decide to pack it up and go away?"

"It did for the mage," I said.

"Uh huh. And we both know he'll be back—or someone like him." Lily shook her head. "You don't want the authorities getting wind of you. Especially the mundane ones."

"I guess," I said. I looked at Lily, eyes narrowed as I voiced my other suspicion. "Still, rather convenient that the wish failed then. It must have been pretty elaborate programming for you to have set that up."

"Wasn't set up. I made the call once I saw it happening," Lily said, confirming my suspicion.

"You can do that?"

"Of course." Lily pointed to my hand and her ring that sat on it. "I'm still linked to the ring. So long as you wear it, I'll always have some awareness of you and your surroundings, ensuring encounters happen logically and according to your wish is part of my job after all."

"Huh," I said, nodding slowly. Well, that made sense, and it was what I'd signed up for. Still, knowing Lily was spying on me was just a little creepy. Then again, after a while I'd gotten used to the great god Google tracking my searches and where I traveled every day. How was this any different really? "Hey, why didn't they do something about my ring? I mean, those guys seemed like the kind who'd steal them."

"The ring has an obscuration enchantment on it. You'd have to be significantly more powerful before you could pierce it," Lily answered promptly.

"Like the mage," I said and got a confirming nod. "Then, El?"

"We walked through her wards into her place of power," Lily said, and I nodded. It still didn't explain why Lily never showed El's level to me, but I left that for now. I'd asked before and never gotten a satisfactory answer.

"We done? Because my food's getting cold."

"Yeah, yeah." I waved her back to her life as I wandered to the pile of quest notes. Might as well check out what else she had found.

Chapter 10

Life continued in this rather sedate and mundane fashion for weeks. I picked up a couple levels as I expanded my understanding of magic, learning more complex ward spells and a pair of new spells, Glamour and Illusion. It might have seemed they were the same, but glamours affected living creatures while illusions, inanimate objects. Due to a living being's natural aura, illusions were not a viable form of concealment, often breaking down before long upon interaction. Glamours, which interacted directly with the aura of a living being, were much more effective and actually altered the perception of viewers. Of course, both of those statements only held true for someone at my level; Lily had been quick to stress that powerful and skilled mages were able to cast illusions on living beings and glamours on inanimate objects as needed.

Still, I had fun playing with both spells. I often added an illusion to my messenger bag and a glamour to myself before I left for the day. Something small but noticeable—a new logo, a tiny tattoo, or highlights in my hair. Just small changes that allowed me to practice the spells without costing me too much in terms of concentration or energy, which was another major thing. These spells had to be continually channeled, like my Heal spell.

Nearly a month after I'd acquired them, nearly four months after I had acquired the ring, a new incident occurred. I should have expected it really.

After all, the secret of the ring could not be kept forever. It was as I was walking out of the hospice building, after a grueling day of healing, that she confronted me. Six feet, two inches tall—towering over my diminutive five-eight—blond hair, and green eyes, the Amazon-escapee leveled a spear at my chest which I nearly walked into.

"Mr. Henry Tsien, hand over the ring or face the judgement of God!" the blonde said, spear held unwavering in front of my chest. Clad in a weird mix of armor and a nun's habit, blond peeking out from the edges, she couldn't have been older than her late teens at best. She might have held the spear competently, but her high voice and slightly breathy tones did little assure me she was serious.

"Oh, hell…" I muttered, staring at the woman. I raised my hand slightly, pushed against the blade, and frowned when it refused to budge. Well, this looked like another social encounter. Surely I wasn't expected to fight a crazy, spear-wielding nun in the middle of the streets, right? While the hospice building was somewhat out of town and in a quiet neighborhood, it still wasn't exactly inconspicuous.

"Do not blaspheme!"

"Seriously? You're holding a spear and telling me not to swear?" I goggled at the woman, shaking my head at the insanity of it all. "And don't you people have something about not attracting attention?"

"Innocent bystanders have been dealt with," the woman said.

I frowned and looked around, noticing for the first time the way the area around us was filled with a golden yellow light. I stared at the light, some of the ways it interacted with the surroundings tickling at my memory.

"Now, hand over the ring."

"No," I said as I stared at the light. On closer inspection, it wasn't diffuse in a solid format but had shades to it, and within those shades, there were gradations of that golden power. I frowned, for the harder I focused on the light, the harder it was to see it. On a hunch, I unfocused my gaze and watched as the image snapped into place. "It's a— owww. Why'd you hit me for?"

"You are ignoring me!" the blonde said, almost stamping her feet, pulling back the haft of the spear that she'd smacked my shoulder with.

"Imagine that. I'm ignoring the crazed person holding a spear at me who seems to think hitting me is going to make me do what she wants." I shook my head. Looked like my hunch was right; she wasn't actually going to hurt me. "Did your parents never teach you manners? You could at least introduce yourself before demanding things from me. Or hitting me."

"You… I am Alexa Dumough, Initiate of the Knights Templar, tasked with the retrieval of the ring you wear on your finger," Alexa said, her spear returning to point at me.

I glared at the spear as I rubbed at my injury and parsed her words together. "Huh. I thought the Knights Templar were disbanded—something to do with the King of France? And initiate? Is that lower than a squire?" Now that she had finally introduced herself, I noticed the information above her head populate further.

Alexa Dumough (Knight Initiate Level 8)
HP: 80/80

Now that she'd hit me, she'd gained an HP bar. That wasn't good. The only time Lily ever made that information appear was when she thought I would need it. Still, it did seem Lily was expecting me to have to fight Alexa, a factor I was not in favor of. It had nothing to do with the fact that she was a girl and had everything to do with the very sharp spear she held.

"I am… you, the ring! Give me the ring," Alexa finally snapped, prodding the spear forward.

I jumped backward, my eyes wide as the tip nearly pierced my chest. "Are you insane, woman!" I snapped at her, my eyes wide as I reflexively patted at my chest. "You could have—" I frowned, feeling something wet and sticky on my fingers. I looked down, seeing blood slowly trickle down my chest. "Oh, you did."

"I… I'm sorry! I didn't mean to." Alexa gasped, dropping her spear as she rushed forward. "Here, let me—"

"Stay back!" My hand raised reflexively as I called upon and cast a Force Spear, ensuring that I blunted the newly upgraded version of my offensive spell. It hit her head on, and she stumbled as she tried to stop herself, the blow catching her on the forehead instead of chest as I had planned. The sickening crack and the sudden weightless slump had me wide eyed. I lurched forward to catch her but had to abort, the nerves in my chest finally sending me delayed pain signals.

Legs giving way under the pain, I sank to the ground and pushed back against the flowing blood. I drew a shallow breath, focusing on the Heal spell as I tried to slow my bleeding via magic and pressure. Damn it. She had barely even pushed the spear forward. How had it cut through me that easily?

The Heal spell formed and then faltered, fading away before I pushed back against the failing spell structure, reforming it in my mind. Mana flowed, more than I could use, spilling from my control as I channeled the spell into my body. I could feel my blood twist and shift, slowing and congealing while new cells grew, forming at the edges of my wound. Pain, subdued at first while I'd concentrated, exploded as my body worked to heal itself. My spell faltered and failed, and it took long, agonizing minutes before I could piece the stab wound together again. This time, when the pain came, I was ready for it. I rode the waves of pain, coasting along the edges of blanking out before the world resolved itself into a persistent headache and my mana depleted.

I pulled myself out, running fingers along the gummy and sore wound, glad to see it had stopped bleeding. It had not healed, but at least the wound had closed. Good enough, at least to get back. However, as I stared at my chest and the bloody mess that was my shirt and jeans, I had to wonder how the hell I was going to get back home. Thankfully, I had an extra pair of clothing on me, but still…

A slight groan near me had me looking up, frowning as the blonde stirred and reminded me I had another problem too. I slowly inched over to the girl, pushing the spear away from her hands before I patted her down, quickly locating a wallet with her ID and some cash and nothing else. I frowned, staring at the money and the blonde, brain turning.

****

Thank God taxi drivers had a tendency to not ask questions when you paid in cash. Of course, it helped that the illusion I cast on the spear helped reduce the strangeness of it all. Still, I was grateful when I finally got the blonde into my apartment. Her dead weight dropped unceremoniously on the floor, and I sagged against the wall.

When I finally came to, I found Lily sitting next to me and Alexa trussed up with some rope. I blushed slightly, realizing where Lily had found the smooth, silk rope, not that Lily seemed to have noticed. I might have been having a dry spell right now, but I did have interests outside of my books.

"Henry, why did you bring her back?" Lily asked grumpily.

"I couldn't just leave her there unconscious!" Moving gingerly, I crept over to Alexa and cast the Heal spell on her, only to be surprised that she had almost fully healed with nary even a bruise. Weird. Still, I hoped that meant she would be fine and no permanent damage had been done by knocking her unconscious. Unlike in the movies, knocking someone out often meant you had given them a concussion, which in the real world had severe consequences. On the other hand, the way she had healed, perhaps we weren't exactly in the "real world" as much. I was still working out how much the supernatural world changed the reality that I'd known before.

"She's an initiate with the damn Templars. And there was an illusion spell all around you that she certainly didn't cast," Lily said.

"Fine. I wasn't exactly thinking that clearly. Something about getting stabbed…" I frowned and then turned to the spear. A few minutes later, some furious scrubbing and a liberal application of bleach had ensured the spear was clear of any blood. That didn't help with the blood that had spilled in front of the hospice building, but at least this kept it out of her hands right now. Eventually, the blood would lose its efficacy as a link, thank God.

By the time I was done, Alexa had finally woken up and was sitting up. Surprisingly, after an initial struggle with the rope, she seemed perfectly calm, first checking her surroundings before fixing me and Lily with a serious look.

"I will warn you that I am trained to resist torture of all forms," Alexa said calmly.

"Torture?" I said, dumbfounded before I shook my head. "Hey, I'm not the one who did the stabbing!"

"You just knocked me out and kidnapped me," Alexa said.

"What? You'd prefer if I left you unconscious on the ground?" I asked.

"Yes."

"Told you so," Lily said, smirking at me.

"Traitor," I said to Lily before I fixed my gaze on Alexa. "Now, how the hell did you learn about the ring? And why you?"

I frowned as Alexa sat there in silence, glaring at me. While I waited, Lily walked back toward her computers, yawning slightly behind her hand. Alexa followed Lily's movements at first before she turned back toward me and caught me looking her over.

"Stop that," Alexa snapped at me.

"Sor—you know what? No. I'm not. You stabbed me," I snapped back and crossed my arms as I glared at the girl. "And looking at you to make

142

sure you aren't going to stab me again isn't something I'm going to apologize for."

"You weren't checking the ropes, and I can't even move anyway," Alexa said, jerking her arms and making her breasts sway slightly as she did so. "You were being a pervert. I can see it in your eyes. Sister Mary was right—all of you men are perverts!"

"Hey!" I protested, though she was right. I had checked her out, but hey, I was a man. And I wasn't doing anything to her and wouldn't either.

"Well, come on then, violate me already."

"What kind of sick world did you grow up in? I'm not going to do that," I said, shaking my head.

"Oh, yeah, that's what you say now. Why else would you kidnap me?"

"I. Am. Not. Going. To. Rape. You," I snapped at her.

"Prove it."

"How?"

"Look into my eyes. I'll activate a skill of mine called Lord's Judgement, and it'll tell me all the sins on your soul, including your dirty, perverted thoughts," Alexa snapped back at me, and I growled.

"Fine!" I leaned forward, still making sure I was out of her reach and met her gaze.

"The Lord's Judgement." Alexa's voice had changed, gaining a timber and depth that resounded through the room. For a second, she seemed to glow with that same golden light I had seen at the hospice building. Time seemed to stretch as our gazes met, my consciousness seeping into hers, before she blinked and said, "Ewwwww."

"Wha…" I leaned back, dizziness slowly disappearing.

"Sister Mary really was right," Alexa muttered.

"Really, we're back to that again?" I asked, rubbing at my temples. "I thought your damn skill was supposed to tell you the truth?"

"Yes. It did. And I'm never doing any of that with you," Alexa said, shaking her head and looking confused. "But… you're not a bad person."

"No shit," I said and then frowned, my brain finally catching up with my emotions. "Wait, you just tricked me into letting you cast that skill on me, didn't you?"

"Finally!" Lily said, smacking the top of her forehead with the palm of her hand. "You really aren't very good at this, are you, Henry?"

"He really isn't," Alexa confirmed, smirking at me. Well, I guess I'd have smirked too if I was tied up, recently concussed, and still managed to trick my captor into… well, something. "I don't believe he actually fell for the 'innocent girl' trick."

"He's a bit of a white knight," Lily confirmed, shaking her head slightly as she continued to play on the computer.

"I'm surprised you didn't stop it though, Jinn."

"Just a spectator here mostly," Lily said. "Anyway, you seemed to have things well under control."

I growled at the pair, dragging their attention back to me. "Again, why the hell are you after the ring, and how did you know about it?"

Alexa frowned and coughed slightly. "Maybe I'd talk more if I had a drink?"

With a sigh, I walked toward her with a glass of water, keeping a close eye on Alexa. She took her time sipping on it, finally sitting back to indicate she was done. I put the glass away and sat back down to stare at her while she smiled at me.

"You wouldn't be willing to let me go too, would you?"

"No."

"Girl has to try," Alexa said, smiling slightly. It was interesting that she seemed a lot more confident here, tied up, rather than when she'd held the spear to me. I'm sure it said something about her, but what I couldn't say for sure.

"You going to answer? Or are you still playing for time?"

"Not completely oblivious, are you?" Alexa asked, and at my raised eyebrow, she shrugged. "Fine. An oracle we use learned about the ring being found. They saw you, the ring, and the city and said I had to be the one to come. And no, I don't know why me."

I grunted, keeping silent. I understood why; anyone else and they'd have been out of level and wouldn't have been able to interact with me. If I had to worry about oracles and other seers learning about the ring in this way, I had a feeling I could expect a lot more visitors soon.

"So now what?"

"I thought that was my question," Alexa said back, wiggling slightly in the ropes again to emphasize her point.

"Well, are you going to stab me again if I let you loose?" I said, frowning.

Alexa lips pursed as she turned away, her voice growing faint. "I'm sorry."

"Sorry?" I asked.

"Yes. Sorry. I didn't actually mean to stab you yet." Alexa raised her voice. "I'm sorry, all right? I, well, the martial track wasn't my thing."

"Martial track?" I frowned, and Alexa pursed her lips, shaking her head. Right, of course. Secret society so they obviously had their secrets. Still, I could guess easily enough—there were probably different ways to serve the society, and she was probably more administrative or social. Maybe magical? "So, stabbing is a no?"

"I…" Alexa paused, her voice firming. "My task is to ensure that the ring does not fall into the wrong hands. I will ensure that the scourge that is…" Alexa's voice trailed off as she stared at Lily, the scourge of the earth who had a lock of hair in her mouth as she clicked away happily at her computer.

"Right, right. Stabbing still on the table. We'll talk about untying once it's not. Now, I'm hungry." I stood and walked to the kitchen to finish my own meal. It was only when I had brought and set the plates on the table, rice and quick stir-fried beef bowls that were ready on the kitchen counter, that I realized one rather important issue: we didn't have enough space in my bachelor pad to all eat—not at a table anyway. "Well, I'll eat first then."

"What if I gave you my parole?" Alexa asked, raising her voice.

"Hmmm?" I asked around a mouthful of rice, staring at the blonde.

"What if I gave you my parole that I wouldn't run, attack you or the jinn. Will you untie me then?"

"How do I know you're telling the truth?" I asked after I swallowed. The look Alexa shot me could have sent me under if stares could kill.

"I swear in the name of the Lord and my hope of everlasting salvation that if I am released, I shall not attempt to escape, attack you or the jinn, or otherwise act against your interest for the duration of this night, so long as I am treated with the respect and care as befits a prisoner," Alexa intoned. Again, she was sheathed in that golden light, and then it was gone, and it was just her green-eyed stare, fixed on me, waiting.

"Ummm…" I paused and looked over at Lily, hoping for some help. However, the jinn was studiously avoiding my gaze. Right—GM couldn't give advice. However, in this case, a non-answer was as good as an answer since I knew Lily would have tried something if she really thought this was dangerous. At least, I believed so. "I'll retie you just before we sleep. Deal?"

At her confirming nod, I released Alexa, who immediately stood and headed for the washroom. I felt a twinge of panic, knowing there was a window she could escape from that I'd forcibly pushed down. If she left, it might actually be for the best. I wasn't entirely sure what I was going to do with her as a prisoner anyway.

"Lily, magic question. I keep seeing this golden light whenever Alexa invokes something. I'm assuming that's another form of mana or magic? Faith magic maybe?" I asked.

"Bingo." Lily smiled at me. "Faith magic uses a different power source than your spells—the power coming direct from the gods they believe in."

"So, God is real?"

"Real enough to power her spells. Though that could be said the same for many others," Lily said.

I opened my mouth to ask for more clarification, but the door opened, and Alexa walked to the table to grab her bowl. Not ideal, but at least I had an idea about what she had done.

Dinner, not surprisingly, had been awkward. Attempts at conversation—or interrogation, as Alexa had called it—failed spectacularly, crashing like a burning blimp. In the end, I ended up

148

spending the last few hours of the evening reading through my spell book while Alexa ran through a series of stretches before submitting to being tied once more. A simple ward spell on the rope helped satisfy me that she would not be removing it without alerting myself. Then, I dealt with the next problem—bedding for the night. A few quick reconfigurations, and I was on the floor next to the door, my sleeping bag rolled out while Alexa slept on my bed and Lily played on the laptops.

As I tossed and turned on the floor, I kept returning to my new problem - what the hell was I supposed to do about Alexa? I couldn't exactly release her since she'd be coming back to try to take the ring from me. But I certainly couldn't just hold her prisoner. If nothing else, my bachelor apartment was going to get extremely crowded rather quickly. Even as I drifted to sleep, no answers came to me.

Who would have ever thought that among my problems after becoming a mage would be the care and handling of a prisoner?

Chapter 11

"For the love of all that is holy and unprofane, get her a toothbrush and let her bathe," Lily whined the next morning, a hand held over her nose.

"I—"

"I give you my parole as I swore last night but for the day. Please, hurry. I would like not to soil myself," Alexa said, eyes wide as she crossed and uncrossed her legs again and again.

"Okay, okay," I said, stumbling over to let her loose. Once released, the woman shifted her body so fast I could have sworn she had a spell on her. The got-to-go-to-the-potty spell. While Alexa was busy cleaning herself up, I set to getting breakfast ready. Which in this case was a pot of coffee and three-day-old bread toasted and covered with butter and jam.

"Decided what you're going to do yet?" Lily asked as she looked up from the laptops. I shook my head as I brought a cup of coffee for Lily, who gratefully took it and handed me back an empty cup in return. I grimaced as I deposited the used cup in the sink and leaned against the cupboard, thinking over my options once again.

There really were only four: kill her, imprison her, let her go, or get her to give up her mission. The first option was a no go for obvious moral reasons, and well, imprisoning her was just a delaying tactic. I had to let her go really, if I couldn't convince her to give up retrieving the ring. The question was, how? That thought consumed me as I finished breakfast, a never-ending series of inane ideas—bribery, blackmail, logic, and blackmail.

"Will you stop staring at me?" Alexa asked finally, exasperated.

"Sorry. Just thinking," I said.

"About me?" Alexa perched on the only other chair in the room while I sat on the bed and Lily clicked away. "Decided that your best option is to kill me yet?"

"Seriously, what kind of training did you get?" I asked, exasperated. "I was trying to work out how to convince you to give up on taking the ring."

"Not going to happen," Alexa replied, shaking her head. "That ring—the jinn—is too powerful to be allowed to go unchecked."

"Yeah, because Lily over there is really dangerous. I think she just about cracked level eighty with her sub," I said dryly.

"That—" Alexa grimaced and shook her head. "She might be contained now but only because the ring constrains her power. If she were to be set free to do what she wants—"

"I'd continue to play these games. Maybe get a library card. Visit a few cities and some old friends. Bud and Merl are always good fun. It's been ages since I've been to Peng Lai," mused Lily as she continued to play.

"And I'm supposed to believe that?" Alexa said, her voice filled with scorn.

"Of course not. I was more telling Henry here. Give him a few ideas for trips when he levels up a bit. It'd do him good to meet some of my friends," Lily replied and looked at Alexa, smiling slightly. "Some of your people could do with meeting them too. Perhaps it'd convince you that the world isn't ending anytime soon, no matter what you think."

"That's because we keep you supernaturals in check!" Alexa snapped, to which Lily snorted and looked up, fixing Alexa with that thousand-year-old stare she occasionally got. I watched as Alexa paled, the weight of the look enough to quiet the initiate.

"Please. You do good work, but the real heavy lifting is done well above your paygrade," Lily said, shaking her head. "Not that anyone actually does much anymore. Mostly, it's just another cold war."

"I thought there were, you know, gods that just wanted destruction. Ragnarök, the apocalypse, 'eating the sun' kind of things," I said.

"Oh, yeah, there are those idiots, but they're locked down pretty tight. Any time they poke their heads out, the others give them a good smacking," Lily replied. "It's amazing what globalization has done for the general stability of the world. Once everyone got over the fact they weren't the only ones, dealing with the idiots became so much easier."

"That's rubbish. Look at World War I!" Alexa refuted Lily.

"Yes. Let's look at World War I," Lily said, tapping at her computer for a few seconds before focusing on us. "A giant world war with guns, tanks, and other newly revealed forms of destruction. And yet, no islands sank, no dark gods rose or civilizations sent back to the dark ages."

"A few million people died!" Alexa said.

"People die. Civilizations die. You get as old as most of the people you're worried about are, you accept that fact. We're not here to stop you from doing stupid things, just destroying the world," Lily said, shaking her head. "Most of us actually like this world and the way it is. Do you have any idea how boring an ice age is?"

Alexa opened and closed her mouth before she glared at Lily, falling silent. I watched the pair for a moment more before I cleared my throat, drawing attention back to me. "Anyway. Lily isn't a threat right now. She's stuck watching over me because of my wish, and I don't intend to destroy the world."

"Even if I believed that, I can't let you keep it. There's nothing to stop someone else from taking the ring," Alexa said.

"Except the Mage Council already tried." I paused, making a quick decision. "Your oracle, they sent you to fight me and not someone more senior, right? Did you ever wonder why?"

"Well... yes." Alexa frowned.

"Right, well, look..." I leaned forward and gave her the gist of the matter. I noticed Lily twitch, but

154

I ignored it, deciding to gamble. I told her all about it, how combat with me was restricted by my wish, how I would eventually get better, but till then, the truly dangerous could not touch me.

"You're saying I was chosen because I'm as good as a four-month-old wizard?" Alexa asked when I finally wound down.

"Well, ummm…" I paused and looked over at Lily who had returned to her games. "Not exactly me—"

"No. It was your game system. Which is controlled by the jinn," Alexa said and pursed her lips. "And according to you, the Mage Council has already tried and failed to take the ring."

"Yes."

"You know, you're not exactly making your case here," Alexa replied. "Sooner or later, someone is going to manage to take it from you. Over your dead body if they have to."

"Says the woman who stabbed me," I muttered, and Alexa flushed.

"I said sorry already."

I shook my head again, the initiate a contradiction of emotions and reasoning I had yet to understand. She wanted the ring but felt bad about almost killing me. Yet, if I had to guess, without her parole, she might try again. Then again, if I thought about the entire religion, I could see how the contradictions inherent in her position could be difficult.

"What do you expect me to do?" I growled, throwing my hands up in the air. "I can't stop people from coming after me. We tried to keep this quiet, but it seems like not talking about it doesn't help. I'm doing the best I can."

"It's not enough," Alexa said, her voice growing soft. "You have your wish, and you'll be a full mage. But so long as you have the ring, you'll be a target for forces you cannot control. Give me the ring and let us handle the problem."

"And what would you do with it?" I frowned, staring at Alexa and tapping the ring with my thumb. "Are you going to lock it away? Or use it?"

"I—" Alexa paused, then spoke frankly to me. "I don't know. That is a decision that will be made by others more senior than me."

"Right. And all of them are going to be wise and smart and not try to make a wish," I said. "You said it. The ring, Lily, she's too powerful for others to use."

"You did."

"And I actually talked to her before I made my wish," I said. "And even then, look at the shit I'm in. Wishes have unintended consequences. Always."

"I'd also point out that so long as Henry lives, my strength is seriously curtailed," Lily said, pointing to me. "His first wish is quite strong and requires a significant amount of my strength to function. Even if he gave you the ring, it would be significantly less powerful. And it wouldn't help

156

him; the Mage Council would not believe he gave up the ring voluntarily. Nor would any others that might come for it. And even once they were convinced, many of those that would come would kill him anyway to reduce future competition."

"Exactly." I nodded firmly and then paused, running the last sentence through my mind and paling slightly. "Anyway, the ring with me means we won't get stomped immediately. No guarantee with you guys."

"We are Knights Templar. We are not, not, not a nerd living in a basement bachelor suite with his gaming books and tame jinn!" Alexa snapped, standing up and glaring at me. "We have God and the Church on our side and can protect that ring."

"Except you didn't, did you?" I asked, shaking my head. "I found the ring in the belongings of an ex-Mage Council member, so you guys must have failed before."

"It was hidden from us. That the ring resurfaced, after so many years… we cannot, I cannot, let you have it, Henry. Once my parole is up…" Alexa shook her head. "I must keep it safe. Even if I have to kill you. I will not hesitate next time."

"And there we have it," I said, flopping down on the bed. "There it always ends up. All the preaching about love thy neighbor, turn the other cheek, be peaceful and pacifist. That always gets thrown away for the damn god of practicality."

"And you don't subscribe to it," Alexa said, pointing at Lily.

"Well…" I laughed, shaking my head. "I don't go about telling everyone else how to live. Also, I made a wish to gain magic powers. Whimsical and foolish seems to be more my wheelhouse. And yes, I'm a little bit of a dreamer because I'm not giving this ring up."

Alexa opened her mouth, but I refused to look at her as I continued to stare at the ceiling. For all my whining and complaining, she was right. The Mage Council, the Knights Templar, and god knows who else were coming. And so far, they'd played nice. I might have been protected, but everyone else around me wasn't. Even I could see the damn hole in our defenses. There was nothing I could do to stop them, so…

If I couldn't beat them, I'd change the rules.

***

"Lily." I squatted next to her and waited for her to look at me. I gestured to her games, and she raised an eyebrow, tapping to put them on pause or at least let her guildmates know she was gone. Seated on our only other chair, Alexa looked up with interest from the book she was reading. I ignored her, and she made no move to come closer, though she was obviously listening as I continued. "I have an idea."

"And I'm not going to like it," Lily said.

"No. But I think, well, this might work. I'm assuming I can't wish you free, right?" I nodded to the ring, and Lily's confirming nod let me dismiss that option. Not that it was very high on the list. For all that I liked the jinn, she was also someone I'd known only four months, and I would admit I was a bit of an optimist when it came to people. Fooling me would not have been hard. "Figured. Right, then we do the next best thing. We make it so the ring isn't available to anyone even if I die."

"How?" Lily asked as she raised an eyebrow.

"Well, I was thinking the sun?"

"No," Lily said, shaking her head. "Anything above the earth would spark a war among the gods. The agreements that bind them from interfering would be void."

"And under the ocean is probably a bad idea since, well, I'm sure there's Atlantis and merfolk and the like, right?" I said.

"No Atlantis," Lily said, shaking her head. "Seriously, it was just a story, but you humans…"

"Huh." I paused, assimilating that fact before moving on. It wasn't as if I could do anything about it. "So, we'll need to find a place which can't be accessed by mortals easily, preferably hidden, and that the gods won't fight over. Sound about right?"

"It'll also have to be after you're dead," Lily said. "So long as your initial wish is active, the link between myself and the ring can be easily traced."

"Right."

"You are going to make the ring disappear?" Alexa said, finally breaking in. "Think of the good it could do."

"Oh, please," I said, shaking my head. "Haven't you been listening? The ring, Lily, isn't a solution. She's just another damn problem. No offense."

"A little taken," Lily said, with a smile.

"But to make it disappear..." Alexa said, shaking her head. "Won't you trap the jinn too? Put your 'friend' in whichever location you decide on?"

"Yes." I closed my eyes and then reopened them, and Lily tilted her head to the side, her face carefully blank as she regarded me. "I think it's time for you to go."

"What?" Alexa said, startled.

"It's time for you to go. Shoo. Your parole is still active, but I don't want you here. You don't need to know the details of this wish," I said, my voice firming. "In fact, it's best if you don't."

Alexa crossed her arms in front of her body. "I—"

"Alexa, go. Either that, or I'm going to knock you out." I raised my hand as I began to call a Light spell to hand.

"You'd be breaking your side of the bargain," Alexa said, eyeing the glowing light above my hand warily. After all, while most people knew what Light spells might look like, there was no guarantee it was not hiding something else.

160

"So are you," I said and then paused, looking at Alexa straight in the eyes. "Please. Just go."

Alexa hesitated visibly, seeing something in my eyes that finally made her nod. She quickly gathered her things and left. At the door, she hesitated for a second, searching for something more to say. But we'd said it all, again and again.

When we were alone, I turned back to Lily, who had arranged her face into a careful, impassive mien. I smiled grimly and then tapped her on the nose, making her blink. "Well, that should work. So, here's what I was actually thinking…"

Lily stared at me, her eyes widening before they tightened, crinkling slightly. She leaned in as I lowered my voice to get her feedback on my second wish.

***

"What did you do?" El snapped at me when I finally opened the door for her. She stalked in, pushing me aside, and looked around the apartment. It didn't take her long, at which point she spun around and stabbed me with her finger. "Where is she?"

"Lily?"

"No. The other super-hot jinn who lives with you," El growled.

"Huh. You find her hot?" I raised an eyebrow and then yelped as El stabbed me in the chest again with her finger.

"Stop playing around, Henry. This is important," El said. "What did you do?"

"I solved a problem," I said, pushing her finger away and closing the apartment door. When I turned back to El, she had her hip cocked and arms crossed. "Lily's busy letting the relevant people know what I did, as per my wish."

"And what did you do?" El asked. "Because what I'm hearing is less than encouraging."

"I made a wish that will guarantee no one gets the ring if I don't die fulfilling a level-appropriate challenge after level one hundred or from natural causes," I said.

"Why?" El frowned, looking at me.

"Because if I just made the ring disappear after I died, they'd have no reason not to kill me immediately. In fact, I'd be begging them to do so. This way, they have a time limit and a goal—get me powerful enough to die without the ring disappearing," I explained.

"That just puts a target on you and lets these groups know the ring has been found," El said, staring at me.

"It was going to come out anyway. I've been attacked twice—"

Her hand rose, and El's voice grew chilly as she asked, "Twice?"

"Oh, right. You didn't know. Well, you see…" I quickly explained about Alexa to El, who gritted her teeth through the entire explanation.

When I was done, El smiled at me sweetly, leaned back, and kicked me in the balls. At which point, she ended up hopping on her other foot, cursing up a storm, as her foot had come in contact with the wish. When she was finally done, El was seated on my bed rubbing her shin.

"Next time, call me!" El growled.

"I had it under control. No one died," I said and shrugged. "Anyway, Alexa was nice, if kind of single-minded. She wasn't about to kill me."

"She stabbed you. And told you she would do whatever it took to get the ring!"

"Well, sure. But that's just her job," I said, waving my hand. "Anyway, now she won't."

"Did you just make a wish to get in her pants?" El said, her eyes wide.

"No!" I replied instantly. After a moment, I continued slower. "Look, Alexa was just the tip of the spear. The next person to come along wouldn't be as nice. I needed to make sure they wouldn't try to kill me or, you know, threaten others to get to the ring. This way, I get people like the Mage Council and the Templars watching over me so that when those idiots do arrive, they get dealt with."

"Why would they—" El paused, a chain of possibilities probably running through her mind. Outside of a few groups that would want the ring gone, any power-hungry group would actually be lining up to guard me.

"And what happens if you fail before you're level one hundred?"

"Well, then I'm dead, and it ain't my problem," I said. "But seriously, before level one hundred, I'm as safe as I can be. After that, well, they'll likely just give me a bunch of idiotic quests in an attempt to kill me."

El nodded, her long hair swaying. "It sounds well thought out mostly. But if they know about this, aren't you worried they'll try to work out the limits of your wish? Or a way to beat Lily?"

"It's a risk," I said, agreeing with her. "But it's better than doing nothing. And so long as I can level up at a decent rate, the chances are low."

"And when you die?" El finally asked. "The ring becomes the property of whoever can get it."

"Yes," I said, smiling wryly. "But I've no intention of dying anytime soon. And who knows, maybe I'll figure out a better plan by then."

"You better. We don't need another damn war," El said, shaking her finger at me.

I could only nod. After all, I had no intention of causing one either.

Chapter 12

After El had left and Lily returned, life once again returned to its prior routine for a few days. The only real change was that Lily rarely used the second laptop anymore as she was forced to pay greater attention to me and our surroundings. Since we hadn't wanted to alert everyone, we'd instead worded the wish such that she could and would check my surroundings and the buildings regularly for new interested parties. This allowed her to impart the warning before they started making trouble. At least, that was the theory.

Of course, that left me stuck up at home for the most part till everything and everyone settled. Not that I wouldn't need to head out and grab some quests again soon enough—if for nothing more than to pay rent and build up some reserves. I hated not having any real cushion, but between the numerous failed and unpaid quests and my unemployment before this entire thing, my emergency fund was looking pretty anemic.

Which made the pounding on my basement door one morning rather surprising. I frowned, peeking through the peephole to see a grumpy-looking Templar initiate with a bag slung over her shoulder standing on the other side of the door. I cautiously opened the door, noting her spear was at least capped and covered. Still, I put up my Lesser Shield first too.

"Yes?" I said.

"Let me in. This bag is heavy," Alexa said as she pushed against the door. It banged against my foot and stopped, bouncing back slightly. "Well, come on."

"The last time we spoke, you threatened to kill me," I said.

"Yes. And then you made your stupid wish, and now I'm to help you survive. So, let me in," Alexa said, pushing against the door harder.

I winced as the pressure increased against my foot, and I finally moved it away. The blonde stomped into the room, dropped her bag on the ground, and then spun to me, leveling the still-covered spear at my chest.

"Let me make this clear. I'm here to help you get to your level one hundred without dying. After that, you're someone else's problem. We're not friends. We're not even allies. We're just people with sort-of-similar goals."

"Actually, I think—" I stopped as the spear stabbed toward me, stopping a good distance away but making its wielder's point. "I get your point. But what makes you think I should trust you?" I said, crossing my arms in front of my body defensively.

"How do you intend to stop me from following you? Tie me up?" Alexa said bitingly.

"Well..." I leered at her and ducked quickly as she swung the haft at my head. Okay, I deserved that. "You know, following people who don't want you is known as stalking."

"Then you should have given the ring up when we told you to. The Brothers are watching you now, following your every move from a distance. And I'm sure there will be others soon."

"And you're what, the inside girl?"

"I'm here because I was ordered to," Alexa snapped. "Now, where do I put my stuff, and what is our first… quest? That the term?"

"Ugh. Fine. Let's find you a spot," I said while still eyeing her spear and wondering how the hell we'd handle having a third person in this apartment. At least Lily and her mystical nature seemed to skip many of the more unpleasant aspects of a mortal body. I was pretty sure I wouldn't be as lucky with Alexa.

Ten minutes later, we had her meager belongings placed next to the pile of clothing that Lily had managed to acquire on the floor. I grimaced as I made a mental note once again to look into finding a shelving unit that might work.

"No, no, no," Alexa growled as she flipped through the quest papers next to Lily. "Is this what you've been sending him on? There's no way he'll hit this… this… level one hundred with these quests. Cleaning a boat's hull? How is that even a quest?"

"It's a Viking longship that has traveled the waters of the seven realms," Lily said calmly. "You might find the barnacles a bit more challenging than you'd expect."

"Garbage!" Alexa said, growled, and tossed the paper away. "How can you justify sending him on these quests? He's a wizard! They wield the powers of creation at their fingertips, and you have him running errands like a handyman!"

Lily paused, eyes fixed on Alexa, before flicking her gaze to me and then returning to the initiate. "Well, he's been by himself thus far. No one to help pull him out of trouble if things go bad. So, yes, we've been picking safer quests that might be slightly below his level."

"I knew it!" Alexa crowed. "Give up the good stuff, Jinn."

"Whoa. I never said I was forming a party with you—" A pair of incredulous looks made me shut my mouth. Fine, yes, letting her in was pretty much my way of agreeing to this entire endeavor. But it would have been nice to be asked anyway.

"So… you're joining a party with him, right?" Lily said as she shuffled some papers around and pulled a smaller stack out. When Alexa reached for it, Lily refused to let the papers go till she received a firm nod of agreement. "Good. Then—party screen."

Alexa Dumough (Initiate of the Knights Templar Level 10) has joined your party.
HP: 120/120

"Aaargh!" Alexa staggered and dropped the sheets, holding her head as Lily invaded her body with her spells. I stepped forward for a second and then paused, stepping back. No telling what she'd do if I got too close, and a small, petty part of me couldn't help but cackle at her pain. I might have still been holding a little grudge over getting stabbed. Eventually, her breathing ironed out, and she looked up and waved her hands in front of her face. Alexa's face scrunched as she stared into the air, her eyes shifting and lips moving as she read something silently.

"Huh. Do I look like that?" I asked rhetorically. In the corner of my eye, I could still see the mini-portrait of the blonde and her health bar if I focused.

"Yes. Except dumber," Lily said.

"Thanks."

"This is your character screen thing, isn't it?" Alexa said, her face returning to normal as she turned to the two of us. "It's… infernal."

"No. Jinn," Lily said. "I should add that since you're in the same party, you cannot hurt each other intentionally. At least not for the first attack. After that, you'll be automatically booted from the party."

"No surprise attacks," I said, nodding to Lily in thanks. Smart girl.

"I'm not going to kill him. I'm here to make sure he doesn't die," Alexa growled as she collected the papers from the ground, pulling one off a plate filled with half-eaten pizza. I noted that her hands still shook slightly, but otherwise, the woman was back to business. Lily crowed in happiness when the plate was discovered and snatched the pizza slice to consume it, much to the disgust of the blonde.

"This should work," Alexa said after she perused the information a little more and thrust a piece of paper at me. "Accept it and let's go."

"Uhh…" I paused as I read over the details. "This—"

"Accept. It," Alexa snapped at me.

I ignored the glare she gave me, reading over the quest notice one last time. It was level appropriate, I guessed, if more dangerous than what I was used to. However, Lily was right. We'd been lowballing the quests lately to make sure I didn't die. If this was level appropriate, then adding Alexa to the team should work—assuming she was telling the truth.

And I'd admit I found it hard to doubt the initiate. Not only because she was so damn straightforward, but because the entire point of the second wish was to create a situation like this. Any good role-player would tell you that you can't complete the really challenging quests without a good party. Still, I asked a few questions of Lily before I finally found myself accepting the quest. I took a little pleasure when Alexa jumped as the quest notification appeared in front of her eyes without warning.

Hey, I'd take my wins where I could.

***

"This your car?" I said, envy in my voice. It was not as if it was a Ferrari or Lamborghini, but the recent-model blue hatchback staring at me was significantly better than my feet and occasional bike.

"Not mine. It's the Templars'. You sure you don't have one yourself?" Alexa said as she got in. A few seconds of fiddling with the insides and the GPS and we were ready to leave for our first party mission.

When the silence in the car finally got too uncomfortable, I spoke up. "Maybe we should talk about, you know, the party before we get there."

"What's there to discuss?" Alexa asked. "We get to the woods, you locate the Kallikantzaroi, we kill them, and you level up."

"Is that what they teach you in knight school?" I said, surprised at the cavalier way she discussed the upcoming confrontation. I had actually hoped for more guidance. When silence just greeted my query, I frowned and looked over at the initiate. "Alexa?"

"I'm not a knight, remember? I'm not even a squire," Alexa said, her voice cracking slightly. As I stared at her closer, I realized her grip on the wheel was tighter than it needed to be, lines of tension running along her forearms and shoulder.

"Shit," I said, realizing she had told me that before. I suddenly wondered if we could change the quest. "What did you learn?"

Alexa's lips tightened before she continued, eyes focused on the road. "I'm decent with the spear and have passing knowledge of other melee weapons. I'm familiar with guns too, but we were meant to receive more intensive training later. I can be trusted not to shoot myself, but I would not be confident in wielding one in combat. I, well, I was specializing in faith healing."

"Faith. Healing." Doubt crept into my voice. "That thing where the hacks put their hands on people's heads and then shove them backward and say they're cured? And hope the placebo effect works?"

"We are not fakes," Alexa said, anger tingeing her voice. "I was learning to open myself to the power of God himself. Did you ever stop to wonder why so many still go to such events? If it was all fake?"

"I thought it was because people were idiots," I muttered.

"No. Just hopeful," Alexa said. "Many of our members move among such groups, providing what aid they can. It's not much, but it is what we can do. Other groups, other sects, have a much larger presence than Knights Templar."

The way she said the last, I got the feeling I wasn't getting the rest of that story. Or why a woman who looked like a professional wrestler would prefer to be a healer than the fighter she was built to be. Then again, who was I to complain about people playing against type?

"I guess monster combat wasn't in the curriculum?" I asked finally.

"No, the squires would have studied that," Alexa said, and I nodded slowly. Right. Right...

"Well, if that's the case, I might have a few ideas..."

***

Boarded windows with graffiti, sidewalks that smelled of piss and other unmentionables, and paint that wasn't new two decades ago greeted us as we got out of the car. Alexa locked the doors behind us, though we were more likely to have the wheels stolen if anyone was still around the neighborhood. Mostly though, the industrial complex was abandoned, too far away for most transients to live and too worn down for businesses to run after the manufacturing businesses that had been the lifeblood of the complex left. The few businesses that were here were best left unquestioned of what they actually did out here.

Even for such a place, the presence of a Kallikantzaroi clan was too much to bear. After a few pointed questions to Lily, I had confirmed that the quest had to be an extermination quest—no bargains, no deals, just death. A few more queries explained why—you didn't make deals with the Kalliks because they never upheld their ends. It had less to do with an untrusting nature and more to do with their notoriously short memory spans. You couldn't uphold a deal you couldn't remember.

Alexa took the lead once the car was parked, her spear under a light glamour to make it look like a, well, long stick. I would rather have made it disappear, but simple was better in this case. Removing the spearhead was simple and effective. A woman carrying a long stick around might raise questions but wouldn't automatically draw the police.

We walked through the industrial complex for about thirty minutes, circling worn buildings and looking for signs of the supernatural. Well, I looked for signs of the supernatural. Alexa just looked. I saw no wards, no shields or other magical markings to indicate which building the Kalliks were in, but Alexa eventually led us back near where we'd begun.

"There." Alexa pointed at a metal window grating with her spear. Upon closer inspection, I realized the grating was only held together by some well-placed bent nails. As I stared, I also realized the grass around the region was just a little thinner, sparser than the surroundings, and the window itself cleaner.

A few moments of jiggling and we had the grate off the nails, allowing us free access to the basement of the building. Alexa squirmed in first, dropping softly to the ground and moving aside to allow me to follow. The sparse light that filtered in from the dirty windows was still sufficient to show us we'd entered an old, empty office space. The mushy, moldy mattress we had landed on was the only sign of civilization. If you could call it that. A single closed door led out of the room.

Alexa moved forward carefully, placing an ear against the door and holding still. I stood back, forming a Force Spear in one hand while I layered the Lesser Shield spell in front of me. That spell, along with its equivalent ward placed on the jacket I wore, were my only forms of defense. Unlike me, Alexa had a full set of modified armor under her coat, a mixture of Kevlar and chainmail links sewn together cunningly, such that the armor barely slowed her down—or was noticeable beyond a general bulkiness.

After a short time, Alexa moved away from the door and shook her head. I assumed she meant she had heard nothing, which meant little. Once again, I wished I had a better grasp of my magical abilities. It should have, in theory, been a simple matter to cast a spell to draw noise to me. It was just a simple application of force after all. Still, in the middle of a quest was not the place to be experimenting, but I did make a mental note to test the idea for next time.

As we had no other options, we got ready to open the door. A few moments of frustrating pantomime, and another few hissed words, finally had our entry worked out. I stepped forward to open the door while Alexa ducked in immediately, spear held in front of her on guard. A moment later, I slipped in and closed the door behind us. Silence and darkness greeted us, and even as our eyes adjusted to the gloom, we still could not see far ahead.

"Light," Alexa hissed softly, and I had to agree. It might give away our position, but we needed to see. A quick pair of Light spells later and we had a couple of bobbing lights tethered to our bodies. A quick thought had me peel some loose paint from the door and slide it into a back pocket. Who needed breadcrumbs when you had a Link spell?

The light spell showed us an empty basement vault of the old manufacturing building. We had come out on a small landing, the room dropping another ten feet beneath us, filled with abandoned and rusting machines. Metal arms, hunched over snaking roller conveyor belts, dotted the floor, breaking up our sight lines.

The silence of the abandoned plant was broken by the scratching sound of nails on concrete and the slow swish of feet being dragged against the ground. In the distance, yellow eyes glinted from reflected lights as more and more of the Kalliks awakened.

Quest Update: Clear the Kallikantzaroi clan from their lair.

You've located the Kallikantzaroi clan but have alerted them of your presence. You'll need to defeat their warriors before they can be convinced to leave.

"Shit," I whispered and then realized that we weren't hiding anymore.

"Yes. Maybe we should have thought about this a bit more," Alexa said as she hefted her spear and readied it. For a moment, I considered suggesting backing into the other room, but here we had the advantage of high ground, assuming the Kalliks didn't wield any ranged weapons.

Throughout our short conversation, the Kalliks had continued to approach. At the edges of my light spell, they gathered, yellow eyes catching and reflecting the light. On instinct, I reached for my mana again, splitting my concentration a third time. I felt the mental strain and was grateful that this spell was simple. A quick gesture and the Light Sphere flew out and hung a good twenty feet away, exposing the Kalliks fully.

Hunched over in groups of five or so, the Kalliks were squat, black-furred creatures with the arms of a monkey and long donkey ears across giant heads. Sharp, curved claws caught my attention immediately as the creatures hissed at the additional light. Instinctively, I threw my other hand forward, my Force Spear arcing through the air at my command as I attacked the monsters in front of me. Something in my gut, in my hindbrain, said that these creatures weren't something that could be reasoned with or talked to.

The Force Spear was almost invisible in the meager light, the distortion in light that marked its position barely visible. The Kalliks in the direction I'd gestured twisted and shifted by reflex, but they were not paranoid enough, not until the spear landed and pinned one of their friends to the ground. The screams and roars reverberated through the plant and set my teeth on edge.

"Wha... WARN ME," Alexa snarled as she hunched and set herself as the Kalliks, spurred forward by my attack, charged us.

"Sorry!" I muttered unconsciously and focused on forming another Force Spear. Seconds, precious seconds I took to create the spear. Kalliks covered the ground before us impossibly fast, and by the time my spell was ready, the first one was halfway up the landing.

A single, beautifully executed lunge later, and the Kallik was dying on Alexa's spear. The blonde initiate's face was fixed in a snarl when she stepped back and yanked her spear out of its body, already turning to face the next attacker. A hasty block caught a swiping claw on the spear shaft before Alexa retreated to give herself room and swept the spearhead in front of her in an attempt to keep the creature back.

The clatter of claws against metal near me caught my attention, and I glanced down, seeing the broad, smashed nose and donkey ears of a Kallik near my feet as it hauled itself up above the metal railing. I gasped, brought out of my reverie, to stab with my formed spell. I kept the spell formed in my hand as the motion punched a hole in the monster, black blood flowing from the newly formed wound. A hasty swipe bounced off my Shield before I thrust again and released the spell, the released Force Spear tearing the monster off the landing.

Beneath my first attacker, another was clambering up, ready to attack. I snarled and raised my hand, channeling Heat as I thrust my hand downward. A roar of flame and a throbbing headache appeared in conjunction, and I played the improvised flamethrower over the landing and my attackers. The Kalliks released their grips, dropping down low in fear.

Without time to form another Force Spear, I relied on my first offensive spell—Force Bolt. It was not as powerful as Force Missile or Spear, but it had the advantage of having an extremely short cast time. Hands held out before me, I even abandoned my Lesser Shield so I could form spells faster. The next few minutes became a blur of gnashing teeth, glinting yellow eyes, and swiping claws as I battled to keep the creatures from climbing the landing directly while Alexa killed those that dared challenge her.

As I spun to the side again, after releasing my latest Force Bolt, a hard swipe tore at my arm. Concentration broken, my spell dissipated as I stumbled backward, pain radiating from the injury. The low-level Force Shield woven into my jacket fabric saved my arm from serious damage, but as the Kallik swiped at me again, I had to throw myself backward to escape its attack. The railing hammered into my back, bringing a sharp exhalation of breath, and I stared as the Kallik raised its claw, ready to tear my throat out.

A too-human scream jarred the Kallik's concentration, making it hesitate for a fraction of a second. A thrown spearhead punched through its neck and interrupted its attack for all time. I exhaled in relief as I clutched my arm and turned to look down the landing to see Alexa as she stood weaponless and bloody amid the corpses of her attackers.

"Tha—" The ankle that was yanked out from beneath me sent me falling forward abruptly, cutting off my voiced gratitude. I landed hard and bit my tongue, blood immediately filling my mouth as a forgotten Kallik pulled itself upward, using my body as leverage. Claws pierced my skin, and I jerked spasmodically, my feet kicking out uselessly.

By the time I recovered my senses fully, the monster had squirmed two-thirds of its way through the railing, its claws dug into my feet. I slapped a hand sideways at its head pitifully, short, coarse hair and the flexible cartilage of an ear coming into contact with my skin. My hand closed around its ear as claws continued to dig into my body. I twisted and yanked upward, jerking the Kallik toward me and away from my prone body.

A moment later, Alexa was there, as she tackled the monster and sent both of them into the metal railing. Alexa snarled as she plunged a knife that I never knew she had into the monster while I pushed myself away. Seeing that Alexa had things mostly under control, I tried to form a Heal spell around the radiating pain of my wounds, but the spell formations and chants escaped my grasp with each pulse of pain.

***

I came to as a warm energy pulsed through me. As I returned to wakefulness, I noticed the pain from my wounds was gone, replaced by this comforting, warm feeling. As I attempted to sit up, I found an insistent pressure on my chest and a noise in my ears that finally resolved into words.

"Stop moving!" Alexa said and pushed on my chest again. "You'll open all your wounds again."

"Sorry," I said as I relaxed onto the cold floor again. Unable to feel my wounds as that energy flowed through me, I instead focused on my own Heal spell, letting the initial portion of the spell play through my mind. That part of the spell focused on locating injuries and assessing the damage, a magical feedback on the extent of damage that I had experienced.

The overall results were not good. I had numerous cuts and stab wounds in the back of my legs and a few in my torso, from the last Kallik that had clawed itself up me, along with the cut in my arm. Add to that numerous scrapes and bruises and significant blood loss and I was grateful

Alexa's healing ability was patching me up. Unlike my own spell, it seemed to bypass minor things like blood loss and instead proceeded to fix problems directly, using the energy as its fuel source. Still, I decided not to just wait for her to be done and focused on my own spell, searching for and directing the spell to focus on the production of additional blood.

It took another few minutes before Alexa finally let me up. By that point, I had begun to shiver slightly from the cold, lack of movement, and blood loss and had to spend the next few minutes doing jumping jacks and chugging an energy drink. I resolutely kept my eyes off the Kallik corpses during this entire process.

"Did we complete the quest?" I asked Alexa while she looked on with an amused expression. I had to admit, between the blood stains, torn clothing, and low light, I probably was an amusing sight. Still, the movement was at least warming me up.

"Not yet," Alexa said. "I'm pretty sure I heard a few others moving around afterward, moving away from us."

"Okay, well, I'm ready," I said, my spells formed in my hands. It seemed a side effect of her spell was a reduction in the headache and mana weariness I experienced from casting. Before we left the landing, I spent a few minutes adding Light Spheres all around the building. Even with the added light, we saw no further signs of trouble in here.

A short and tense hour later, we had searched and prodded our way through the entire warehouse and were finally sure the Kalliks had left. A broken lock and a few fallen treasures on the way out the door told a tale of a hasty retreat. I was glad. The other signs we found indicated there had been children here. I knew I had to get harder, but killing children, even monster children, was a line that I couldn't cross. Not yet at least. Perhaps it was because they were humanoid, or that they seemed mostly sentient, but the thought of murdering them just didn't sit well with me. The quest complete notification, as usual, was just more information that we already knew. This time, Alexa only shifted a bit when it appeared.

"What are you doing?" I blinked as Alexa returned to the main nest of the Kalliks and sorted through what was left.

"Searching," Alexa said. "Ah, har!" She pulled out a wad of cash which she pocketed. A few minutes later, she had some jewelry and some other, more questionable, acquisitions. Some, I could guess, were reagents, items that people like El would like.

"Isn't this…" I frowned, searching for the word. "Wrong?"

"They left. And they probably took these off people they killed. So, no, I'm not finding it wrong," Alexa said. "How do you think the

Templars finance themselves? Killing monsters isn't exactly government funded."

"Oh," I said, wondering exactly how much money you could make looting dead bodies. Then, I considered my own circumstances. "You going to share?"

Chapter 13

In the four months since I had acquired the ring, I had gained all of seven levels. In the following four weeks after Alexa moved in, I doubled my level again. There were a few reasons for this. Firstly, I was no longer struggling to figure out the new world I lived in, spending as much time questioning Lily and El about the world as I was questing. Secondly, the newer, tougher quests that we worked as a team forced me to constantly push myself, while Alexa's constant, nagging insistence on training when we weren't questing increased my productivity. Even if I hadn't been slacking off, the woman brought a focus to my training that hadn't been there before.

Not all our new quests involved violence, just a good portion of them these days. As we learned from our mistakes, we started spending a greater portion of our time studying and learning about our potential opponents before we embarked on the quests. Between Lily's extensive knowledge and the Templars' archives that Alexa was able to access, we rarely walked into a problem ill-prepared once we actually started doing our homework.

Thankfully, even Alexa understood that constant violence was a bad idea. Every couple of days, she would pick out a challenging, if nonviolent, quest to undertake. I had to admit, these quests were my favorite and ranged from spending a day layering warding spells, under the guidance of a master warder, to being magical security at a rave. I even managed to put my very first personally crafted spell into play at the rave as I muted the music all around my seat while I watched for glamours and illusions being used to sneak the underage in.

Five months after joining the supernatural world, as I lurched out of bed and got the coffee started, I had to smile as I pulled out my new character sheet.

Class: Mage
Level 14 (45% Experience)
Known Spells: Light Sphere, Force Spear, Force Shield, Force Fingers, Alter Temperature, Alter Sound, Gust, Heal, Link, Track, Scry, Mend, Ward, Glamour, Illusion, Detect Magic

I'd grown quite a bit in the last few weeks, and even if I'd never admit it to Alexa herself, it had mostly to do with the initiate. Of course, I wasn't the only one who had developed. Alexa had grown more confident, sure of herself and her choices during the quests. The continuous training she did in the mornings had honed her martial skills.

What puzzled me at first was that Alexa would also sneak out regularly at night or when we had called it a day. One particular evening, I decided to spend some time scrying her, using a piece of her hair, my familiarity with the woman, and a clear bowl of water. Unfortunately, once she entered the office building that was her goal, further scrying attempts were blocked. I'd admit I felt a little dirty doing it, but considering the precarious situation I was in, I felt it necessary. In the end, I spent time watching the office building and Alexa, coming to the conclusion she was reporting in to her superiors. That the office building was within walking distance of my apartment was both reassuring and suffocating. In the end, all I could do was put the entire thing to the side.

The coffee beeped, finally telling me it was ready, and I poured myself a cup before turning to the side to look at the jinn. "Lily," I called and waited for her to pause her game before I continued. "We need to talk. About my sheet."

"Oh?" Lily said inquiringly, arching one perfectly plucked eyebrow. Or shaped? Created? After all, the visage she showed was entirely artificial. I thought. I wasn't entirely sure about that, come to think about it. "What's wrong?"

"The spells. Or skills. Or, you know, this entire thing," I said. "The knowledge you are inserting into my head is beginning to diverge a bit from what I see here. Or maybe the things I understand are diverging. It's like I've got these spells in my head, but as I understand them, as I level, I realize each of the spells are just parts, components. I can alter them to do what I want if I want. Well, theoretically at least."

"Good."

"Good?"

"Of course," Lily confirmed. "It means you're beginning to understand magic properly."

"But, if these spells don't matter…" I frowned, shaking my head, trying to explain my concerns.

"Listen, Henry. Learning magic is like learning a new language. People like myself, the fae, vampires, and the kraken, we're native speakers. We grew up knowing magic, and while we might not necessarily know the finer points of grammar, we intuitively understand it and can 'speak' the language. Humans though, you're ESL. Most mages learn magic step-by-step, memorizing words and understanding the rules of grammar. It means they aren't as intuitive as we are, but they can sometimes pull off things we would never have thought of.

"You on the other hand, well, you're different. The way you're learning magic from your levels is closer to what I understand—intuitively, as a whole. But at the same time, you're human. You need to understand the rules. The spells, well, they're like memorized chapters from a book. You know the chapters and can speak them without thought, but to really understand magic, you need to analyze each sentence, each paragraph, individually."

I nodded at her words, rubbing my chin. If we took the analogy further, there were words, concepts Lily had inserted into my mind that didn't necessarily "fit" with any of the spells at first glance but actually underpinned why the spells worked. I could cast any of these spells, and even alter them, by changing specific words or adding new paragraphs. In fact, I'd been doing this without really considering the underlying structure of the spells.

"Does that mean I'm just a giant parrot? Squawking away spells whenever I need to?" I asked.

"Yes," Lily said, smiling slightly.

"Huh," I said. I'd have felt insulted, but the fact stood that I didn't understand the majority of the spells. Even my Light spell, which was perhaps the easiest spell I knew, was something I still could not cast without relying on the gifted knowledge. But the spell was more complicated than willing light to appear. First, you had to define what light was, then you had to define how much mana you'd supply to create the light. If you were creating a light ball, you had to define the space that the light itself would be in, which meant defining the sphere that the light energy was being focused into. Then, you had positioning of the spell itself in relation to yourself and the world. And that was for the simplest option, without adding in modifications for ongoing channeling and tethering of the spell to yourself.

The Force Bolt was even more complicated. The spell was actually a wave of built-up kinetic energy shaped into the form of a dart, locked into space by mana, and then propelled forward by even more mana. On top of all the size, shape, and energy definitions and power requirements that the Light Ball required, Force Bolt also needed to be defined according to its flight path and patterns. Still, if you looked at it that way, upgrading the spell from Force Bolt to Missile was simple. I was mostly just altering the shape of the container with minor adjustments to the amount of force wielded. The Force Spear, on the other hand, was more complicated with a significantly larger container and more complex equations required as it traveled and interacted with the real world.

"We done?" Lily asked, interrupting my thoughts.

"Not really. I still think the way we have this set up isn't good," I said, waving my hand. "Maybe we should have started with a different system. Perhaps one that did better at teaching the basics."

"Just remember," Lily said. "You're asking me to try to teach you magic when I use it subconsciously. It's only because I've been owned by so many mages in my time that I even know where to start."

"Yeah, I figured," I said. "Still doesn't solve the problem."

"Well, I could put concepts into your mind and let you work it out from there," Lily said. "Hopefully you'll figure it out?"

"Uhhh… no," I stated firmly, making Lily laugh. Before we could continue the discussion, the doorknob twisted and opened, reminding me that once again, I needed to get Alexa her own key.

"I'll think about it," Lily said as she turned back to her game. "You know where the quests are."

Alexa frowned slightly and shot a suspicious glare between the pair of us. When she received no further clarification, she walked over to pick up the quest sheets. Still, from the line in her back, I had a feeling I was in for a more difficult quest.

***

Sometimes, being wrong was worse than being right. In this case, rather than a difficult quest, Alexa had located a monotonous, boring, and yet exacting quest—the unloading of a container's worth of magical merchandise. As the merchandise couldn't be physically touched, I spent the entire day moving one box after the other with Force Fingers, also known as an abbreviated form of magical telekinesis. Of course, added to the dull, throbbing pain from the constant use and concentration required from magic, I also had to contend with the icy disapproval radiating from Alexa. Not that 'anything was wrong' when I'd asked of course.

By the time we got home, I was ready to curl up on my makeshift bed and sleep the night away. Unfortunately, Lily had other ideas. Once Alexa had stomped into the bathroom, the olive-skinned jinn waved her hands at me, and a series of words appeared.

Magical Skillset
Mana Flow: 2/10

Mana to Energy Conversion: 2/10
Spell Container: 2/10
Spatial Location: 3/10
Spatial Movement: 2/10
Energy Manipulation: 2/10
Biological Manipulation: 1/10
Matter Manipulation: 0/10
Duration: 1/10

"Wha…" I said and then stopped, my sluggish brain finally catching up with me. Of course. This was Lily's solution to my problem. A series of skills that demarcated my knowledge. Still. "Why out of ten? And what's considered good?"

"Ten because I'm not doing percentages. Again, jinn, not a god. I can't read your mind, so these are rated off your shown understanding of magic," Lily said. "And an apprentice mage would be expected to be a three across all these areas."

"Ah." I frowned, prodding at the list before adding, "This an arithmetic or a logarithmic increase?"

"Logarithmic, I guess. It's going to get harder the more experienced you get. Not that information you need changes, but how easy it is to learn it," Lily explained.

"Thanks," I said. Well, at least this helped to solidify some of the concepts I had been playing around with. As I lay on my mattress, I could not help but prod at the list to get further information.

Mana Flow dictates your control of mana—the amount, quantity, and quality of mana you can put into a spell.

Mana to Energy Conversion is a ratio and indicates the quality of your control when converting mana to energy to affect the world. Required for most spells.

Spell Containers define the boundary of a spell. Higher levels of this skill indicate increased complexity and types of containers that may be defined.

Spatial Location defines the location that a spell may be cast. Low levels indicate the ability to cast spells within touch range. Additional levels dictate distance a spell may be cast from the caster and by visual or other methods of defining locations.

Spatial Movement dictates how a spell will or will not move. Higher levels allow spells to adjust trajectories after being cast or to define multiple variables.

Energy Manipulation indicates the caster's ability to manipulate different types of energy. Low levels indicate base understanding of energy types and forms. Higher levels will allow caster to manipulate multiple forms of energy at the same time and rarer types of energy.

Biological Manipulation indicates the caster's ability to interact and understand biological changes. At the most basic level, caster is able to sense and replicate biological

---

matter from a healthy template. Higher levels allow the caster to alter the template, allowing replication from damaged or unhealthy biological matter or the creation of new biological matter.

Matter Manipulation indicates the caster's ability to interact and understand matter. Low levels allow the caster to replicate matter from templates. Higher levels allow the caster to alter the template, allowing replication from damaged matter or the creation of new matter.

Duration dictates the caster's knowledge of time as it relates to his spells. Basic levels allow the caster to constantly channel a spell or to cast a spell of set duration. Higher levels allow longer duration spells as well as the use of time-based triggers for spells.

All of it was self-explanatory really, though some of the hints provided by Lily gave me an idea of the kind of training I needed to conduct. Having a zero in any single area was a bit frustrating, though I had to admit I hadn't actually explored my Mend spell at all. Of course, that line of thinking, that I needed to be a "normal" apprentice with three in everything might just have been wrong. After all, I had spells I could wield without truly understanding them—the equivalent of microwave meals. Perhaps I'd be better off focusing on some other aspects of magic, like Mana Flow. Certainly, if I understood the way my levels worked, part of the reason I'd slowed down in the last week or so was because I needed to be able to physically handle more mana.

I considered the various skills, trying to line them up with the spells I wielded. Perhaps it was time to get a little more experimental...

***

It was dark when I next woke, the only light being the dual glows of laptop monitors, Alexa's unladylike snoring breaking the silence of the night. It was 3:24 a.m. I sighed as I placed my phone down and sat up, debating if I should go back to bed. A loud, insistent growl that erupted from my stomach answered that question.

"Alexa left some dinner on the counter for you," Lily said, not looking up from her monitors.

"Ah... thanks," I said and edged my way cautiously around the room to find it. Pasta. She really liked her pasta. Then again, it was precooked food. After a moment's debate, I tossed it into the microwave while I surveyed my tiny domain.

Tiny. With three people, it was only good fortune that Alexa and I never spent much time at home. Even so, there was little privacy, a fact that had begun to grate on me. Alexa seemed to handle it better, and Lily, well, Lily just played her games. The past few weeks of hard work had actually expanded my meager savings such that I, for once, had some breathing room. Perhaps it was time to find a new apartment.

As the microwave dinged, I grabbed the hot pasta and booted Lily off one of the laptops, content to do some searching. How hard could it be to find a three-bedroom location in my price range?

A few hours later, the answer was: extremely. Unless I wanted to live in a badly serviced suburb, my budget was unrealistic. While questing was an interesting way of generating funds, it was somewhat unreliable. Especially since a good third of my quests refused to complete payment, citing unsatisfactory performance. I'd have complained, but mostly they were right. I was lucky I was still being hired.

As dawn broke, I finished sending the email enquiries to a few potentials and returned the laptop to Lily while I grabbed the quest papers. Best make the selection before Alexa did. As I perused the papers, I was startled by a knocking on the door.

"Expecting company?" I said to Lily, mostly in jest as I walked to the door. Without looking, I swung it open while I said, "No, we're not interested in… what are you doing here?"

Instead of the expected door-to-door salesman, I spotted a familiar tall, sour-faced mage with slicked black hair and a cream shirt.

"You used another wish," Caleb said.

"You here to bitch or destroy more property?" I asked.

"You—" Caleb stopped, drawing a deep breath before he continued more slowly. "I am here to ensure you gain these… levels… of yours."

"At three in the morning? Seriously?" I asked.

"Is it?" Caleb paused, looking around, and shrugged. "Ah, the trans-temporal spell must have been slightly misaligned."

I stared at Caleb while filing that piece of information away. "So, you intend to babysit me?"

"No. I shall teach you the basics of magic to ensure your progress," Caleb said. "I understand you already have a protector."

"Huh. Didn't think you were the teaching type."

"Who is it?" Alexa called out as she stood at the bed, spear in hand.

"The mage who tried to kill me," I replied.

"Move!" Alexa scrambled forward, spear readied before she slowed down as she realized I was just standing there, talking. "Wait. Tried?"

"He's too high a level," I said.

"Oh…" Alexa relaxed and propped her spear against a wall before she walked to the kitchen. "Is there coffee?"

"In the pot."

"As I was saying, I am here to teach you. Now, get your gear, and we shall begin," Caleb reiterated.

"Yeah, no," I said as I turned away and walked into the kitchen. I'd have slammed the door shut, but considering my wishes didn't include property damage, I saw no reason to taunt him that way.

"Do you know what you're being offered here?!" Caleb snapped, his voice rising. "I am a Mage of the Third Circle. Apprentices the world over would sell their mothers for a chance to train under me."

"Is he always this loud?" Alexa asked as she sipped her coffee, eyeing the mage.

"You, Initiate, will be quiet. Or else you will feel my wrath," Caleb snapped. Almost in unison, all three of us rolled our eyes.

"Can't do it. She's part of Henry's party. If you started a fight with her, Henry would have to join in. So, no. She's protected too," Lily said, looking up from her laptops. "Also, you are loud. Can you tone it down? I can't hear the quest log."

Alexa grinned at Lily and stuck her tongue out at the mage. I paused, staring at the blond Amazonian before I chuckled. Sometimes, I forgot Alexa was actually quite young still. Of course, Caleb was less than impressed with us, his brows furrowing.

"Are you refusing my offer?" Caleb asked.

"No." I paused, swiftly considering the matter. Free training, even if it was with someone I disliked, was too good to pass up. And while the wishes weren't foolproof at safeguarding me, the fact stood that I was unlikely to be any safer staying here than going. "I'll take you up on it—in the mornings, when Alexa goes to her own training."

Caleb's lips thinned, obviously unhappy with the result.

"I still need to go and do quests to level up."

Provided with a fitting excuse, Caleb could only nod. "Very well. Let us begin."

***

A short walk later, I was seated in an open-plan office that consisted of a whiteboard, a pair of chairs, and a desk that faced the board, being lectured to by Caleb. Caleb had taken all of fifteen minutes to ascertain my current level of ability and knowledge before waving me to the seat behind the desk. I didn't do particularly well considering it was still in the early hours of the morning and my coffee had only just kicked in.

"Right then, it seems you are entirely ignorant about the world that you have entered," Caleb said. "We will endeavor to rectify that immediately. To begin with, do you understand why the supernatural world has chosen to hide itself from the mundane?"

I shook my head, and Caleb just huffed.

"Of course not. In truth, the question was misleading. We have not chosen to hide; humanity has chosen to ignore us."

"But the glamours and illusions—"

"Are for convenience's sake. Humanity has no desire to deal with orcs, elves, dwarves, or more. They have made this very clear numerous times in the past. Now, those who refuse to hide their visages are dealt with by the appropriate government agencies or otherwise relegated to the outskirts of society," Caleb said. "This process began in the early 1500s and was hastened by the globalization of trade. The Mage Council itself formed during that period as mages across the world met for the first time and the threats we had to deal with increased in proportion."

"Threats?"

"Yes. Threats," Caleb said. "Like your ring, the Never-Ending Gourd, the kris of Hang Tuah. The attacks by the maricoxi or the dokkaebi. Until we banded together, individual mages often found it difficult to deal with these new threats as we had no cultural knowledge to draw upon. Incomplete or incorrect as it may be, this knowledge often holds a glimmer of truth."

"But you haven't explained why the council was put together," I said, and Caleb huffed.

"I would if you would stop interrupting. Do you know how often those with magical ability are found? One in ten thousand. Of those, maybe one in ten have the ability to become true mages. If it were not for the fact that magical ability is passed on genetically, we would have died out long ago," Caleb said.

I quickly did some mental math, coming up with about sixty thousand mages in the entire world. It seemed both extremely high and yet really low. After all, at that rate, a city like mine would have slightly above twenty mages at best. When I turned my attention back, I realized Caleb had continued speaking.

"… safeguard knowledge, watch for other-dimensional threats, and deal with rogue agents," Caleb said. "We are not policemen or other guardians in general. There are numerous other agencies—both official and unofficial, like your Templar, that undertake such tasks. However, experience has shown that certain magical items and artifacts cannot be allowed to circulate in the general public."

"Like the ring," I said, and my lip twisted wryly. "Okay, lecture over. Are you actually going to teach me magic, or are you going to bore me with history till I give the ring up?"

"You—" Caleb stopped and drew a deep breath. "Fine. Let us begin with your Light Spell."

While I wasn't particularly happy to go back and practice such a basic spell, I had to admit it was better than getting a history lesson.

Hours later, as I hurried back to the apartment to grab a bite to eat before we went questing, I had to admit that Caleb was a decent teacher, even if he was constantly surprised by what I did and did not understand. Learning magic from Lily and my own experiments had been a hodgepodge affair with some basic magical knowledge missed. Of course, we didn't cover as much as I had expected since Caleb was of the view that anything that should be covered would be covered. In exacting detail.

Chapter 14

The next day, Caleb was waiting for me at his office at our scheduled time. It was actually kind of nice to leave with Alexa in the morning, having something better to do than practice my magic alone. She, of course, was off reporting and training with her people.

"We will split your lessons into two components. My lectures about the world and theory of magic and, secondly, your practical spell usage," Caleb said the moment I walked in.

"Uhh…" Caught flat-footed, that was about the only word I could utter.

"I will not have any say that even a failure of a student like you was not trained properly by me," Caleb said. "If this is unacceptable, we may call this experiment to an end."

I grimaced before finally nodding. Fine. As much as I hated boring lectures, I had to admit his practical knowledge and ability to pick out what I were missing was particularly helpful.

"Good. Now, if you are to learn magic, you should at least understand the underpinnings of it. There are numerous branches of magic, but to be a mage, one must have a least a basic understanding of it all. It is that broad understanding of magic that separates a mage from other groups like your alchemist friend," Caleb said.

I found a seat while he was speaking, content to listen and remember and take the occasional note. Thankfully, I had a very good memory for important things. However, don't ever ask me to remember your birthday. That was what electronic calendars were for.

"Now, within magic, there are numerous paths—enchanting, evocation, and alchemy being the most commonly accepted major paths."

"What about warding?" I asked.

"A subset of enchanting. The most basic form of enchanting in fact," Caleb said. "Once you grasp the basics of all three, you may begin to combine them into more complex spells or rituals."

"Rituals are hard?"

"No. A good ritual is actually easy to understand and cast. However, to understand and manipulate the workings of a ritual requires understanding of all three paths of magic. It is why the Mage Council recommends that rituals be taught later," Caleb said.

"Ah… and evocation is the casting of spells from mana, right? Things like my Force Bolt and the Light spell?"

"Yes, exactly. Now, if you'd be quiet, I'll begin the overview of each path," Caleb said, glaring at me.

I sighed and fell silent for the moment but made sure to listen. Annoying as the mage might be, he certainly knew his stuff.

***

Within days, we had fallen into our new routine. Early morning, I would make my way to his office, where Caleb would be waiting, a new lesson fully planned out. At first, my constant interruptions derailed the lessons the mage had planned, frustrating both of us. However, once I realized Caleb would, eventually, get to my questions—and if not, he had allocated time for me to ask them— matters proceeded more smoothly. It was on the afternoon of the sixth day that I finally caught up with Lily and had a moment to spare as Alexa was running late.

"Lily, I noticed I haven't actually gained much in terms of experience lately. But I'm sure I'm learning more from Caleb," I said.

"Really? How strange," Lily said, entirely focused on her laptops. However, after so many months living together, I could tell something was not right.

"Lily," I warned, and the jinn sighed, tapping quickly on the computer to put her games on hold.

"I've adjusted your experience gain lately to slow down your leveling," Lily said.

"Why?" I frowned. "Are you worried I'll hit level one hundred too soon?"

"No," Lily said. "Well, not entirely. It's more to do with your body. Have you noticed you've been getting headaches from spellcasting more frequently recently?"

"Yes," I replied. In fact, I was sporting one right now. "I figured it's because I'm using magic a lot more these days."

"You're partly correct," Lily said. "Each time I leveled you, you gained a little more access to mana. Partly from the spells and knowledge I provided and, well, partly from me adjusting the limiters. Remember, you had no real natural ability."

"I remember."

"Right. Well, you're now wielding as much mana as an apprentice mage at times, but your body hasn't had enough time to adjust to it. The headaches are just the symptoms," Lily said.

"Is it dangerous?" I asked.

"No. I noticed the issue early enough, but until your body fully adjusts to the current levels, I'm slowing down your leveling."

"So, you nerfed me," I said, my lips twisting wryly.

"Well, you are the alpha tester for this game. Rule adjustments should be expected." Lily spoke as lightly as I had, though I could see some of the tension had left her body. As if I would get upset about her taking care of me. My third lesson with Caleb had been about magical burnout, and I had no desire to end up a has been. I'd only just started wielding magic!

"How long?"

"Till you next level?" Lily shrugged. "Depends, but at least a few weeks. And you'll continue at this slower rate for a while."

I grunted, unhappy but at least glad to have an answer to the nagging doubt. With this topic exhausted, I went to the pile of quests and flipped through them. I knew Alexa had probably picked one out for me, but I liked to look them over too. It was strange how easily I had given up the responsibility of choosing the quests to the initiate, but in truth, I knew my own caution would have had me choosing lower-leveled quests.

On the other hand, with my current nerfing, perhaps that would have been a better option. Then again, many of the quests we had been doing had more specific financial benefits. It was kind of nice not having to worry as much about my budget, especially with Alexa contributing to the rent.

"Huh." I frowned, staring at the quest paper in hand. After a moment, I flipped backward and located the other quest note.

"Something interesting?" Alexa said from behind me, making me jump. I growled at her while she looked at me blankly. Though as I turned back to the papers, I saw the corners of her lips quirk up.

"Just more Devil Rats," I said. "There are two quests, both around the same area. In fact, I'm pretty sure they're near where I fought the first nest."

"Devil Rats?" Alexa took the papers from my hand. She read through the notices quickly before eyeing the bottom of the paper.

"You know what? Let's go kill them," I said suddenly, pulling the papers away from Alexa and handing them to Lily.

The jinn took them from me and, after a glance, put them back down. Within seconds, new quest notifications bloomed.

"I didn't—"

"You snooze, you lose," I said happily as I walked over to grab my jacket. After a moment's consideration, I went back and packed an additional set of clothing, cautioning the spluttering Alexa to do so as well.

***

The large, abandoned concrete office building that was our objective loomed above us as we stepped out of Alexa's car. In truth, considering a journey into the sewers wasn't required of both quests, the extra clothing and precautions were probably overkill. But since we had a car to store the bag in, I saw little harm in bringing it along. After all, being less than prepared the first time I'd dealt with these guys had been my downfall.

"I still don't get why we had to do a rat-killing quest," Alexa grumbled for the tenth time as she hefted her spear. On my suggestion, she'd brought along a shorter version of her normal weapon. This one barely reached her shoulders.

"Come on, aren't you Templars all about helping people?" I asked. As the job posting had stated, the key for the warehouse was stored in a small, locked keypad behind a bush. In moments, we had the glass doors, that led into the building open. "Ready?"

Rather than answer me, Alexa strode ahead into the sunlit entranceway. Her eyes darted sideways, taking in the disused and empty hallway before she walked farther in. She only paused for a second for me to finish tethering a Light Ball to her.

Light Ball Cast
89% Synchronicity

I was quite proud of how good I had gotten at casting the spell. Not only had I gained a better physical understanding of the motions, mentally I understood why each portion of the spell interacted the way it did. I could, with some difficulty, even cast a Light Ball without the aid of the system. Not that I was going to fool around with that right now.

"Rat droppings," Alexa said, gesturing with her spear as we checked out another empty office. This was our first visual clue that the Devil Rats were here, though the pervasive odor of rat urine assaulted our noses constantly.

"Recent?"

"What do I look like to you? A vet?" Alexa said grumpily before she strode out of the room. Before I could answer, a flash of red in the corner had me flicking my hand out. The already half-formed Force Missile flew directly at the charging rat, spearing it even as it rushed out of the hole it had hidden in. The upgraded spell speared through the monster, maiming it before disappearing.

"Trouble!" I called out hurriedly as I began forming another Force Missile. Behind the maimed rat that was still attempting to reach me, another whiskered offender was crawling out.

"I'm busy!" Alexa shouted back. It was then I realized that squeaks and the familiar swoosh of her spear could be heard from behind me. Had the damn rats tried to ambush us?

"Shit!" I snarled as my next missile missed. The Devil Rat had scrambled out of the way of my cast. It jumped, soaring toward me before it bounced off the Force Shield I swung in its way. Of course, since the Force Shield was an actual shield, I had to carefully control its size. After some experimenting, I had decided to just go with a traditional shield option most of the time and attached it to my left arm. Unfortunately, the jacket's wards just weren't powerful enough for me to rely on solely. Even as I readied another Force Missile, my fingers flying through the complicated motions, I watched the rat before me intently.

"Eat this," I snarled as I bounced the rat off my shield again and tossed my readied spell when it landed. This attack hit, tearing through its body and leaving the monster seriously wounded. Rather than finish it or its brethren off, I stepped backward quickly to check on Alexa.

I might as well not have bothered. Rats, even Devil Rats, were no danger to my Templar friend. While she might have complained about her lack of desire to be a warrior, there was no doubt she had the training and skill to be one. The bloody pieces that littered the hallway were testament to that fact.

"Did they just try to ambush us?" Alexa asked, echoing my earlier thoughts.

"Come on, rats aren't that smart," I said, though my voice was filled with doubt. After all, they were Devil Rats, and even normal wild animals knew how to hunt in packs.

"You ready?" Alexa asked after a moment, and I had to nod. A part of me wondered if these Devil Rats had spread here from the earlier group because I had never exterminated the pack. Then again, how did you exterminate rats? Poison and pesticides, I guessed, neither of which I had access to. Of course, I was once again comparing these rats to their normal counterparts, which might have been a mistake. Sometimes, knowing only a little bit about a subject could be just as hazardous, I realized. I hadn't even taken the time to learn about the Devil Rats from Lily like I had gotten used to doing, so confident that I knew what I was up against.

By the third ambush, there was definitely no longer any doubt what the rats were doing. As we advanced up the office floors, the attacks grew in frequency. That was until we reached the third, and second-to-last, floor.

"We done?" I asked as we finished our walkthrough.

"That should be it," Alexa confirmed as she led us back toward the stairs.

"We weren't attacked," I said, and Alexa nodded again. If they weren't attacking us now, that could mean one of two things: Firstly, we'd killed all the rats there were. The second, more likely option, was that they were reserving their forces. "Perhaps we should talk about how we're going to do this."

Alexa paused, hand on the exit bar, before she turned to me, nodding for me to go ahead. While the fights so far had not been difficult, a little caution made sense.

***

"This is absolutely disgusting," I said as I stuck my finger into the lukewarm flesh of a Devil Rat. I grimaced at the slimy stickiness, the residual heat flowing and wrapping around my finger. "I'm so going to catch something from this."

212

"This was your idea," Alexa said, shooting one last disgusted look at me before she returned to watching for trouble.

"Don't remind me," I said and then shut up. Fingers shifted and moved, my mind stretching down familiar routes.

Link Cast
75% Synchronicity

Scry Cast
64% Synchronicity

Scry link is established.

I felt my senses expand, the link between each Devil Rat letting my mind flow down arcane routes. I frowned almost immediately and pointed to the right. Without hesitation, Alexa's spear flashed out and struck through the drywall, pinning and killing the furry spy. For precious seconds, I struggled with my spell, the split attention almost pulling it apart before I managed to reassert the necessary control. Behind my eyes, a throbbing headache exploded, a pain that at least I was used to by now.

Again, my mind rushed along the link. Above us, on the top floor. Connections. So many connections. I bounced from one to another, keeping count with each skip, the headache pulsing in time. Seconds seemed like minutes, and then I released the spell, slumping against the dirty and bloody wall unconcernedly.

"You okay?" Alexa asked, concern in her voice.

"Mmmmpppphhfff," I replied—or tried to at least. I hung my head low and then blinked as I noted another drop of blood drip from my nose. Shit. I wiped it away and then leaned the other way.

"Here," Alexa said, holding a torn tissue for me. I nodded thanks as I stuffed it into my nose, thinking how silly I looked.

"I counted just over twenty before I lost the connection," I said to Alexa minutes later, when the headache had subsided.

"Are you going to be able to continue?" Alexa asked worriedly.

"Yes. We need to deal with these guys now. I'm pretty sure there's a big nest up there. If we don't do this now, they'll just spread," I said and pushed myself up.

"Too bad we can't just burn the place down," Alexa said, and I snorted. That would have definitely gotten us blacklisted. "I don't think we can take on that many, not the way we've been fighting."

"No. But these floors are all laid out the same, right?" I got a nod from Alexa. "Right then, I've got a plan."

***

The office building was laid out relatively simplistically—the main staircase was behind a fire door which led to a single corridor. Down either side of the corridor were doorways leading to smaller office spaces. From previous experience and the Scry spell, we knew the doorways on the right harbored the majority of the rats. After all, it was along that back wall that the pipes and ventilation shafts ran downward, allowing the rats to move from floor to floor with ease.

When Alexa opened the doorway, I proceeded to toss out the wooden blocks that I had pre-carved the light wards on, having activated them before we stepped in. The wards slid and bounced along the floor, lighting up the hallway even as Alexa dropped another pair of warded blocks in front of the doorway. We then waited, letting our eyes adjust to the brightened room.

As we strained our ears and breathed through our mouths, the light chittering of Devil Rats and the acrid stench of their urine and feces assaulted us. I made a mental note to look into a cleaning spell, or at least a disinfecting one, when I got back before I made myself focus. It seemed the rats refused to come out even with the provocation of the light.

Alexa stepped forward, hands tight around her spear as she edged along the hallway carefully. I followed her, my Force Shield fully cast and extended before me as we eyed the ground for gnawed-through holes in the drywall.

"There," Alexa hissed and gestured with her spear as she spotted the first hole. I nodded grimly, bending down and shifting my Shield aside as I tossed a warded block into it. I followed with a couple more rather quickly, each bearing a simple Alter Temperature spell. Each block was activated to lower the temperature around itself. After a little experimenting, I'd worked out that a single block could lower the temperature of my apartment by a good ten degrees. Putting four in there would start making the entire room entirely too chilly. In time.

Once we had dropped the blocks, both Alexa and I fell back to our prepared line of wards and waited. And waited. And waited. Did I mention that while the wards did lower the temperature, they did so only from the blocks themselves? They basically radiated the cooling effect from their present locations, which in this case meant the entire process would take quite a bit of time.

A half hour later, the rats finally rushed out of the room, obviously done with being frozen. The only concern had been if the monsters had decided to continue retreating rather than launch their attacks early. Fire of course would have been more certain, but again, we weren't about to burn down the damn building. So cold was our chosen weapon of annoyance.

The rats charged us, and the first rat hit the blocks Alexa had laid down, triggering a simple activation sequence. Like the rest of my blocks, the wards had been placed as more of an experiment than with any plan for usefulness. It was only after I had accidentally activated one—destroying the toaster in the process—that I'd decided my blocks might be useful weapons. It had taken a bit of work to get these wards right. Chaining the spell with a touch activation was simple. The tricky part was adding an on/off switch so that the wards weren't active all the time.

Now, as the Devil Rat ran right across the ward, a Force Missile formed underneath it and jutted straight out. The Devil Rat behind it was unlucky enough to cross the ward just as it finished forming, the missile spearing it in the neck. That was perhaps the biggest flaw of the wards—how long it took to form each missile. As it stood, the three warded glyphs scattered ahead of us only managed to kill one and mildly inconvenience another.

"Die!" Alexa snarled, whirling her spear around and cutting in a line as the first Devil Rats reached us. The attack knocked one aside and tore open another. Behind her, I shifted my Force Shield to lie across the floor and grow high, creating an impromptu wall. The leading rats rammed into the Force Shield with a hiss and shake of their heads, momentarily stunned. Above them, Alexa proceeded to stab at the trapped rats mercilessly.

The initial confusion and surprise lasted for a brief second, enough time for Alexa to kill a pair before the rats backed away. The first Devil Rat to jump the Shield wall was battered aside, the second took a Force Missile to the face, and then there was only one charging us, sailing through the air to land on Alexa. The initiate threw herself sideways and sent the rat flying before it could injure her through her armor. Even as the rat scrambled to its feet, Alexa's spear lashed out. I finished off the last injured monster while Alexa was dealing with hers, and then, it was over. A few minutes later, we were all set up for the next room, the cold blocks moved into it after retrieval. Even in the corridor, the chill from the first room could be felt as it slowly dissipated.

The subsequent rooms and fights followed much the same lines—a lot of waiting and a few brief moments of struggle. As my headache grew worse, I made a mental note to create some Force Shield wards for next time. I quickly added a twist to our attacks, setting up a Force Shield just in front of the Force Missile wards. That allowed the wards enough time to form and trigger, adding to the carnage. In turn, Alexa focused on batting the monsters aside as they jumped and otherwise attempted to attack us.

When we finally cleared the building, I was desperately breathing through my nose and attempting not to retch. Blood, guts, and other unmentionables littered the floor, and even Alexa only stayed long enough to ascertain no additional rats had survived before she left. As we breathed in the fresh air outside, I left a message with the building owner about the successful cleaning operation. Of course, a few of the younger rats had escaped into the wall, but those could be dealt with using mundane pesticides and traps.

"Yes, four dozen full grown. That's right. Yes. Okay," Alexa said, finishing her conversation on her phone before she turned to me. Green eyes unreadable as she stared at me, the initiate gestured toward her car.

"Can we do the other quest tomorrow?" I asked as I slid into the car, careful of where I placed my feet. Another throb and my vision narrowed again.

"Headache?" Alexa asked, and I nodded. Carefully. "Tomorrow then."

"Thanks," I whispered, my eyes shut while I dry-swallowed a pair of painkillers. Definitely tomorrow.

***

The headache from overuse of my magic subsided after a night's rest. Rather than go to class the next day, I spent the morning working on more warding blocks. The blocks themselves were simple enough to acquire. While I knew that the better material I worked with, the more powerful I could make the wards, I still went with natural hardwood rather than metal or stone. For one thing, I had no idea how I'd carve metal or stone. Art class in school had at least given me some experience with woodcarving, even if it had been ages ago. More importantly though, I just didn't have the magical oomph to need better material anyway.

Wards were simple enough in theory. A ward could be made of anything from words, characters, glyphs, or runes. So long as the mage focused and provided the underlying magical structure to the ward, you could even use stick figures. Of course, using common magical variations was simple, like walking down a well-beaten path in a forest rather than trailblazing yourself.

Bent over the block with woodcarving tools in hand, I slowly worked the first step into the block. This was the basic empowerment ward which allowed you to input mana into the entire structure. In this case, I was going with a mana storage ward, one of two types that I knew. The other was a constant channeling empowerment ward but, in this case, was much less useful. There were other more complicated empowerment wards, including ones that allowed you to passively collect mana, but I had yet to progress to that level.

Once that was finally carved into the wooden block, and the magical channels layered in, I moved onto the next step. This required me to join the empowerment ward with the spell that it was to power. Of course, to do that, you needed to carve the spell at the same time, which meant setting the parameters of the spell in the ward itself. At the most basic level, I could fix the spell with not-unalterable channels, but it was theoretically possible to create flexible wards. Many protective arrays were actually flexible spells built into the wards.

A ward was closer to a computer program in the way it worked. When creating a ward, you "wrote" the program, allowing for options while writing it. In many ways, wards were like the spells in my mind—they were set constructs that only required initiation. Of course, unlike my spells, which I could alter as I casted them, wards were unalterable except for their premade options. In this case, I was layering a Force Shield onto the wooden block.

It was this analogue that I believed Lily wanted me to experience. Being forced to consider each portion of the spells I had in my mind, and the way they interacted with my wards, developed my understanding of both warding and the spells themselves.

After layering the spell on the ward, I then had to carve in triggers. It was not enough to just have the ward. I needed to be able to control how and when they were turned on, unless I wanted them on all the time. In this case, a simple on/off switch that was manipulated by mana flow was sufficient. All that said, it took me nearly three quarters of an hour to finish creating a single ward. Thankfully, while I was channeling mana throughout the process, the amount I needed to channel was actually quite low, a tenth of what actually casting the spell would require.

It was nearly time for Alexa to get back before I was done with my experimenting, and a series of warded blocks were laid out on the floor next to me. With a flick of my hand, I activated the first and stared at it intently.

"Well, that's a failure," I muttered as I kicked at the Force Shield. While the shield itself held, physics unfortunately took a hand and sent the block skidding backward before it bounced off the wall. The small, curved shield continued to flicker as it ran the stored mana down for another thirty seconds before it died silently. "I need to figure out how to lock the shield and the block down. Though, maybe I could make a bunch of those blocks and link them together? Make a portable Shield?"

"That's a really annoying habit," Lily said from her seat.

"Huh?" I turned to Lily, frowning.

"You're talking to yourself again."

"I know," I said, refusing to apologize. Partly because it was my home. And partly because, occasionally, my mutterings actually made Lily provide a hint or two. In this case, I didn't expect any help. I was pretty certain the required spell formulas to lock the shield in place were too complicated for my current level, especially if I needed to transfer them to a ward.

"Next," I said and carefully reached for experiment number two. This one contained an altered Force Missile. Before I activated it, I cast a

222

Force Shield around the ward, leaving just a little space for me to sneak my hand under it so I could activate the block. A moment later, the block shuddered, and a small Force Missile formed. Rather than actually flying outward, it just sat there, jutting out of the block. A few moments later, I removed the Force Shield and prodded the block, noting it had the same problem. After a moment, I decided to name this block a Force Spike block. It was a mild success; I could create the Force Spike, but like my Force Shield, it could easily be knocked sideways.

I sat back down and glared at my failed experiments. Carrying around some pre-charged blocks to run as a Force Shield might work, but Force Shield was such a mana hog that they just didn't last very long. Perhaps, with more experience and better materials, they might be useful. As for the Force Spikes, they could easily be knocked over, making them useless. Perhaps I could make them caltrops, but then I'd have to either adjust the container to activate, and form spikes around the block itself, or create four different wards.

The incessant clicking of a mouse and keyboard keys interrupted my thoughts once again, and I growled, suddenly tired. Damn it, I wanted my house back. "Can you be quiet?"

"I could if you got me a better mouse," Lily shot back. "And maybe a new keyboard."

"Go buy one yourself. I've got things to do," I said and looked at my ward blocks again, the insistent clacking reaching my ears. Click. Clack. Click.

Oh. Huh. That'd work.

***

"You sure this will work?" Alexa asked later, as we set up for the rats. This time around, we had decided on an entirely different plan of attack. Rather than walking around trying to find the rats, we were going to attract them to us.

"I trust El," I said, nudging a piece of meat a bit farther forward before I uncapped a potion. It was a simple attractant that would target the Devil Rats. It had cost more to get it specifically targeted, but since we didn't want random creatures popping in, we had happily paid for the more expensive potion. Now, I carefully poured the solution on the meat before stepping backward and surveying our preparations. We'd chosen to make our stand at the entrance hallway, with a glass door to our backs, while spread in a semicircle around us were some of my newly created Force Spikes. Ahead of them, chilling the floor and the water we had splashed on the ground, were the cooling blocks, thin layers of ice already forming around the blocks. Hopefully, the slick flooring would slow and disturb the rats enough to buy us some time.

224

"You sure there's only a dozen close by?" Alexa asked again.

"Yes," I replied grumpily while I stood, watching.

"Because if we get swarmed—"

"We won't be," I reassured her. They might be smart enough to plan an ambush, but they wouldn't be able to withstand the lure of the potion—or so El had promised us.

"Ah," Alexa suddenly said, her eyes fixed on red eyes that glinted at us from the shadows. Rather than approach cautiously, the rats rushed us, a dozen in total. Within moments, they hit the icy floor and slid along the ground, their feet desperately scrambling for purchase. A few bounced against the wooden blocks, knocking them about while others scrambled through the gaps to rush us. Two unlucky rats actually stepped on the spikes, the shorter and more condensed spells launching Force Bolts into their bodies before disappearing.

Alexa ignored all this, instead swinging her spear as the rats approached. In turn, I backed her up with tossed Force Missiles, using the spell to harry and injure the monsters that rushed us. Minutes of fur, sharp teeth, and claws and then the battle was done, the rats lying in pieces around us.

"Well, that wasn't so bad," I said as I gulped and waited for my breathing to calm down.

"Good. Because we're going to have to do it again," Alexa said, leveling her spear at another set of eyes.

"Damn."

***

A short while later, we were staring around the mess of an entrance, privately glad we weren't going to be the ones forced to do the cleaning. Alexa squatted a short distance away, washing a few wounds with iodine and verifying she was not further injured. I was keeping watch, grateful once again I had become the backline fighter that I was. Mages were squishy—everyone knew that!

Once Alexa was done and picked her spear back up, I bent down and reached out, recasting the Link and Scry spells in quick succession. A slow, pounding headache began to form behind my eyes before I let the spell go, my lips tight. Damn Scry spell was not getting any easier to use.

"We're clear," I said.

"Good. I'm going to take a look inside," Alexa said, gesturing toward the retail complex. I frowned, my head tilted to the side.

"We're clear," I repeated.

"I know. It's not that," Alexa said. "I just want to look around."

"But—" I clamped my mouth shut as I realized Alexa was already walking in, carefully placing her feet around the puddles of blood and guts. As I caught up with her, I asked, "What's going on?"

"I'm just curious."

"Bullshit," I said. "You're looking for something."

Silence greeted my accusation. Rather than continue my line of questioning, I followed after her and waited for her to answer me. Living with two women for so long, I'd learned a trick or two. We were nearly done with our walkthrough, Alexa pausing at each office to poke around with her spear and light before leaving, before she spoke.

"What do you know about Devil Rats?"

"Big, ugly, red?" I said and shrugged. "Also, I'd rather not fight them again? Smell way too bad."

"Devil Rats are the vermin of the demonic world. They don't appear naturally... mostly. Instead, the demons that infest the rats often come from badly cast demonic rituals, escaping through badly created wards," Alexa said. "Three infestations back to back is... uncommon."

"You're worried someone's summoning demons?" I asked, and Alexa nodded.

"Huh." I rubbed my chin as I poked around further. "So, we're looking for signs of a demonic ritual?"

"Yes. Or other magical ritual," Alexa confirmed, and I sighed. Crap. As if things weren't complicated enough.

***

"Three incidents?" Caleb asked the next morning after I had explained my absence and the quests.

"In about five months," I said. "I didn't detect any other rats though. At least, not in my range." I didn't need to point out how limited my range with my Link and Scry spells were to Caleb of course.

"And you want me to look into it?" Caleb asked, peering at me imperiously.

"You did mention the Mage Council was formed to deal with extra-dimensional breaches," I said.

"Yes. For things on a larger scale. The occasional demon summoned by a wizard is..." Caleb frowned and then shrugged. "Well, it's not something we normally deal with. The local groups normally handle such matters."

"Seriously!?!" I frowned, and Caleb sighed.

"You seem to be working under a misconception. I have already informed you we're not policemen or guardians. The council is more akin to a guild. Many of us have better things to do than hunt down your random wizard."

I glared at Caleb, obviously not happy with his answer. The mage turned away, walking to the whiteboard and tapping on the table.

"Now, we were discussing the sixteen traditional formulas by Kapinsky for the positioning of a spell..."

Chapter 15

As much as I might have worried about the appearance of a demon invasion or two, the next few weeks were uneventful. No more Devil Rats were reported. Even a few late-evening excursions and Scrys had revealed nothing. In the end, it seemed the appearances of the Devil Rats had been coincidental. While uncommon, it was not unusual for the demons that inhabited the Devil Rats to sneak in via cracks in our dimension. They were small enough to do so, and if left unchecked, could eventually wear the barriers away. It was possible that an unexpected shift in the barrier had allowed a bunch of these demons to sneak in. The only thing I could do was keep an eye out for more problems and kill the Rats when they popped-up. Less of them, less damage to the barrier.

During the lull, I even had time to visit a few nice apartments and apply for two. Of course, I then ran into a rather interesting problem—proving my income. I couldn't exactly put "supernatural troubleshooter" or "mage in training" on the application forms, and "secondhand reseller" didn't look much better. In the end, we lost out on both apartments. I couldn't really say for sure if Alexa's insistence on informing the landlords that we were "in no way shape or form a couple" helped or not, but I had my suspicions.

Training continued at the plodding pace that Caleb insisted on forcing on me. I couldn't exactly say the mage was wrong in his training methods as we continued to uncover surprising gaps in what could have been construed as "basic" knowledge. Which was why we were now spending this morning walking the city and receiving a more hands-on education about ley lines and places of power after having spent all of yesterday morning receiving an academic dissertation about them.

"This is a place of power?" I asked, shaking my head as I stared at the side of a building. The mural of a floating space cat with laser beams coming out of its eyes fighting a swarm of green space aliens in superhero costumes was quite creative but not exactly what had come to mind. Wreaths and bouquets of flowers had been laid against the wall along with a single, lonely teddy bear and a scattering of candles.

"Not all places of power are places of worship. Some form due to the deeply felt emotional connection the populace has to a place. The stronger the emotion, the deeper the links." Caleb bent down and placed his own bouquet next to the group. He waved his hand over the candles, lighting them all with a careless gesture of power before he stood.

"So, not all places of worship, but a mural?" I asked.

"No." Caleb shifted some flowers to reveal a picture. "A place of mourning and reflection."

"Ah," I said. A memory tugged at me—a briefly read article about an upcoming musician, his fan base, and a tragic fight. Too young, too dumb to back down. A punch, a bad fall, and the creation of a new legend.

"Now, do you recall why places of power are important?"

"They enhance the amount of mana you can wield. The stronger the place of power, the more mana there is available to use. That lets someone with even a moderate gift wield more mana. It's why some of the most powerful places—the pyramids, the Forbidden City, Mount Rushmore—are always warded and guarded. Don't want a dumb wizard calling up a greater demon," I answered.

"Good. And that's why a competent mage studies every place of power in their city. You never know when you might require a power increase."

"Exactly how many are there? In the city," I said.

"Twelve grade-three, thirty-six grade-two, and one hundred and twenty eight"—Caleb nodded to the mural—"grade-ones."

"Nothing over grade three?" I asked, and Caleb smiled thinly.

"Nothing that you need worry about."

Asshole. Still, as Caleb walked over to the wall, I watched as he began the process of placing wards. We'd practiced it yesterday, but practice and the actual casting were different things. The first ward wasn't particularly complicated since it was an alarm ward. It involved the initial Ward glyph and a pair of Links. The first linked the ward to the place of power and the second to the board that Caleb kept. Of course, the difficult part was the triggers, ensuring the alarm itself would not trigger randomly or due to minor fluctuations in mana flow. While in theory it was simple, in practice, you had to understand not only the power level of that particular point of power but also its normal power fluctuations and the environment surrounding it. It required significant fine-tuning, which made it perfect as a training tool for me.

The second, more powerful and complicated, ward that Caleb cast once he was done with the first was one I had no ability to lay. It basically sealed the place of power, ensuring no one could use it. It was significantly more powerful and complicated. The first ward had taken Caleb a bare five minutes to lay. The second, nearly an hour. The wards glowed for a moment more, visible to everyone before they faded away from mundane sight. Unlike the wards I normally carved out, these were runic wards that were written in glowing mana script. It required somewhat more strength to invert the wards and hide them from mundane sight, but it certainly made things easier.

"Did you see?" Caleb asked finally when he turned to me, weariness etched on his face.

"The first, sure. The second…" I trailed off, shaking my head.

"Obviously," Caleb snorted. "Come, we will have you practice on the next section. And after that, you will take it as a quest of yours. Yes?"

"Yes," I agreed. It was something we had discussed already—a simple quest, one that could be approved by Lily and paid for by the Mage Council. It worked for all of us; I got paid and trained up a spell, and the Mage Council got the places of power that they couldn't be bothered to waste one of their own people on warded. All in all, it worked out quite well. I wasn't entirely certain why they cared to ward places like this since they weren't going to do more than keep watch, but that, when I asked, was none of my business. In fact, I knew Caleb normally wouldn't have sealed this place of power except for the fact that he was here.

As we walked toward the car to head to the next location, I glanced over at Caleb, curiosity warring with my usual social awkwardness. In the end, curiosity won. "Why are you doing this?"

"Hmmm? I'm sure we discussed this."

"Not the warding. The teaching," I clarified.

"Ah." Caleb paused, considering. "It is not as if your wish gave us much choice."

"But why you?" I asked.

"My initial task had not been completed. Until the ring has been returned to the council, I will not receive another," Caleb said.

"Doesn't explain the teaching," I said.

"Teaching you and raising your 'level' is the most optimal route. Once we are no longer constrained by your death, I will acquire that ring," Caleb said simply.

"Acquire. As in kill me," I said, looking at the mage's impassive face. He nodded slightly, seemingly unconcerned with that. "And you're okay with this."

"Many of us have made questionable decisions to gain the power we have," Caleb said after a long silence, his voice calm as he continued to speak. "That yours has constrained your enemies to act at a later date is almost admirable."

"Huh." I leaned back, shaking my head. I guess I somehow had a different idea of what a teacher-student relationship should be. Could be. But then again, my upbringing, my culture, set a higher importance on that relationship, almost valuing it at the same level as a familial relationship at times. To Caleb though, this was just a way of getting me up to speed so he could complete his task faster.

And of course, if he taught me, he'd know all my tricks, which would make dealing with me easier. After all, it was hard to surprise someone who'd taught you. I shivered when I realized that fact. Still, at least it explained the remoteness I always sensed when dealing with Caleb.

***

"You bring a girl to the nicest places," Alexa said as she kicked an empty beer can down the concrete path. I looked up from the ward I was currently placing, considering the desolate skate park filled with empty beer cans, discarded hypodermic needles, and other waste and had to mentally agree with her. This was a shithole and not the worst one we'd seen. After all, locations which were currently occupied were often already warded—by local supernatural organizations or the city. Admittedly, the wards that a mosque or church might use would be different than mine, but they would be no less effective. In fact, most would be significantly more complex. It was thus no surprise that my quest mostly involved dealing with these places—locations that had been abandoned.

"You didn't have to come," I said.

"I definitely did." Alexa continued to walk a circle around me. "My job is literally to babysit you."

"Didn't ask you to," I grumped. Even as I was speaking, my fingers danced as they pulled and stretched at the fabric of reality, and a portion of my mind worked the Ward spell. The days of practice I had received had given me quite a bit of confidence at casting this spell.

"No. I was ordered to." Alexa shook her head. "Child of fate and all that."

"Child of fate?" I frowned, looking at Alexa. "Keep saying that, and I'll get a big head."

"Not you, idiot," Alexa said with a roll of her eyes. "Me. Though how I got tied to you for the next little while, I have no idea."

I worked in silence for a bit since the next part was actually tricky. I didn't have a shortcut for the next part provided to me by Lily, so I actually had to manually cast the spell. While it wasn't extremely different from the Link spell—and in fact, I considered it inferior in many ways—it did have much greater range. By the time I was done, another twenty minutes had finished, and I had begun to perspire. As I stood and wiped away the sweat, I considered the initiate while I rested for a bit. The next part would be even more difficult.

"Care to explain?"

"About the child of fate? It's a term the Church uses to signify people whose presence or lack of it will alter the course of the future," Alexa said. "Telling the future is complicated. Mostly, seers can only see the major events in a person's life— the ones that have the greatest impact on others and places where numerous individuals are affected by an event. A child of fate is someone whose presence occurs numerous times in their visions and whose presence then affects those futures."

"Huh. So, you're not necessarily the agent but a catalyst? Or potentially both?"

"Yes. In fact, I'm not even supposed to know about it. It was only chance that I overheard the abbess arguing with the knights about it when I

236

was a teenager. My choice to become a healer was not taken well."

"Chance or fate?" I said, a slight smile on my face.

Alexa snorted but did not correct me. After all, who knew? In either case, I was kind of glad Alexa had chosen to learn some healing arts. It actually made me feel safer to be with her than if she had been a typical knight.

"Time to get back to it," I said. Within moments, I had extracted the enchanted rods and placed them around the point of power. After that, I began the slow process of linking each rod and activating it. Once the rods were finally linked, the enchantment activated and proceeded to lay out the sealing ward. This was the difficult part since the rods required an external power source—namely me. I grunted as I felt the rods drawing on my gift, pulling mana from me in a steady flow.

An hour later, I finally sighed and relaxed as the rods shut down, the place of power finally sealed. Packing up after that was a simple enough matter, and when I finished, I dusted my hands off and waited for Alexa to fall into step with me. As we exited, I asked, "I have been wondering—what is it with the spear? Why not a gun?"

"A few reasons. Legality to start." Alexa smiled slightly. "You can't walk around with a gun everywhere. Here, I can just say we're part of a medieval renaissance group."

"But it's sharp!"

"Is it?" Alexa offered me the spear tip. I frowned and stared at it, then realized there was a light shimmer to the spearhead. I unfocused my eyes and saw it actually looked to be capped and blunted under the glamour. Huh. Smart.

"You said a few reasons?" I asked, more curious now.

"Effectiveness. Bullets don't hold blessings or enchantments well," Alexa said. "When you have to fight werewolves, wights, or vampires, you really want your weapons blessed. You can't even really use silver alloys. The silver content is so low it doesn't really work."

"And swords?"

"Initiates are not taught the sword till they are formally accepted as apprentices," Alexa said. "Well, not much. We're given the basics, but most of our focus is on the spear till then."

Now that Alexa was talking, I took the opportunity to question her a little more about her life before we'd met. I soon learned Alexa had grown up in one of the many orphanages supported by the Templars. These orphanages were both acts of compassion as well are recruiting grounds where gifted children were drawn into the fold. Once she started reminiscing about her time in the orphanages, the normally quiet blonde started gushing, content to relive happier memories.

In time, our conversation turned into more of a trade. Alexa was definitely curious about my life as an only child in the outside world.

"After that, pets were banned in our house," I said, finishing my story of poor Tut, the turtle. I was still sore about it so many years later. We had arrived at our next and last destination for the day. Thus far, I could only complete three a day at best, often less. "So, what's your guess?"

Alexa frowned as she surveyed the empty parking lot, a single car the only other source of company for us. A short distance away, a twenty-four-hour convenience store was the sole occupant of a strip mall. Once more, Alexa looked around, trying to discern a clue about why a place of power would be located here. However, the empty parking lot gave few clues.

"Must be a ley line thing," Alexa said eventually.

"Mmm…" was my only answer. I frowned and focused my sight. Over time, I had learned I could actually sharpen my mystical sight, allowing me to "see" more of the supernatural world. Spirits, ghosts, ley lines—all those appeared. Of course, there was a price. Within seconds, a throbbing headache made its presence known, but I was able to verify Alexa's guess. The ley line was weird, floating just about twelve feet off the ground before dipping to the earth and pooling at the place of power before sweeping upward again, its shimmering illumination a reminder of pictures of the aurora borealis. As I considered the best way to ward this rather large place of power, a shout interrupted my thoughts.

"Hey, you! What are you doing here?"

The speaker was a rather large, rotund gentleman clad in a T-shirt that depicted a bat tearing free from chains and dripping in blood. I was not able to read the stylized name on the front but had no doubt it'd be some heavy metal band. A lanky man, who desperately needed to wash his greasy long hair, flanked his left while on the right, a short, spectacled South Asian walked.

"Uhh…" I said, feeling caught by the abrupt question.

"What's it to you?" Alexa replied, squaring off with them and jutting out her chin aggressively.

"This is our place," the initial speaker said as he continued to walk toward us. As he neared, his spectacled compatriot suddenly frowned and tugged on his arm, slowing him to whisper in his ear. A moment later, the leader glared at me.

Weird. I hadn't done anything to attract his attention. Beside me, Alexa frowned at her arm where a gold bracelet rested. It had been a recent addition to her arsenal, an enchanted bracelet. When I looked at the bracelet, I noted the glow around the enchantment had increased as it activated. On instinct, I focused on the group and allowed my sight to sharpen.

Faint, so faint I had missed it in the beginning, a low glow of power shrouded each of the individuals walking toward us. I knew that glow. It was the same kind I gave off, like a beacon. Training with Caleb had reduced the glow somewhat, but still, my power overflowed my control. These guys did not suffer that same issue; their power a faint trace in the air. Unlike Caleb, I'd have had to say it was a lack of power rather than great control. I wasn't particularly surprised to see that the glow surrounded all three of them. Those with power, no matter how little, had a tendency to clump together. In a city as large as ours, those with traces of magic had a tendency to find one another, and sometimes, they even managed to form their own baby cults. As Caleb had said, none of them really had enough power to do more than light some candles, but it sure made fooling mundanes easy. Remembering the look Specs had given me, I mentally added "the sight" to their abilities.

"Really? Your parking lot? I hadn't realized that Lumin Parking had hired teenagers," Alexa said.

"You—" The leader stopped, looking at the bag I was carrying over my shoulder and then back at Alexa. "You're the ones sealing off the places, aren't you?"

"What's it to you?" I asked.

"Last warning. Get the hell out of here," Greasy Hair said as the group stopped a bare ten feet from us.

Alexa continued to look bored, though I noted how she let a hand shift to touch the concealed baton in her back pocket.

"Or what?" I asked.

Without speaking further, the pair placed their hands on the rotund boy's shoulders. Within seconds, their leader had begun chanting and moving his fingers, and in the center of his hands, floating in front of him, a small ball of fire bloomed. I had to admit I was a touch jealous. I didn't have a Fireball spell. On the other hand, it took the combined strength of all three of them to cast it.

"Seriously?" I muttered and raised my hand. I recalled my Alter Temperature spell, quickly judged the distance to them, and then cast it.

Alter Temperature Cast
Synchronicity 83%

In a sphere that perfectly enveloped their Fireball, my Alter Temperature spell formed, and I began to forcibly lower its temperature. I watched as the trio gritted their teeth, fighting my spell, but as I had already noted, the trio possessed very little actual oomph. Hell, I doubted they individually registered on Lily's scale of mana control. Within seconds, their Fireball fizzled and died, and the three flinched back together as one as the spell snapped apart. Having failed at spellcasting before, I knew how much it stung.

242

"Nice party trick. Now, scram!" I said. My fingers flicked and twisted, and a Force Bolt formed in my hand, blue-and-white streaks of power running along its edge. This was a pure affectation of course since a properly cast Force Bolt was actually nearly transparent.

"This isn't over!" the leader shouted as his friends backed off, staring at me warily.

I stared at the group and then casually tossed the Force Bolt at them, guiding it to impact the ground near their retreating feet. That was incentive enough to send the trio scrambling away, and I sighed, shaking my head. "Idiots."

"Yes. So, you think they've been coming out here to do dastardly deeds?" Alexa asked, a smile dancing on her lips. "Maybe a few black magic rituals to impress the girls?"

"If they knew any, sure," I said, chuckling. "Keep an eye out? I'll ward and seal this place, and then we can go home."

"Of course," Alexa replied as she settled down to watch.

"Sushi for dinner?"

"Sounds lovely. I'll make the call."

Chapter 16

Over the next eight days, we continued to fill the requirements of our quest. Using a simple city map, we worked inward from the outer bounds of the city, tackling the more remote places of power. We'd finished just over twenty locations and spotted our teenage stalkers twice more. Since they only watched us from afar, we never took any action. Of course, after the second time we saw them, I reported their presence to Caleb. Unsurprisingly, the mage dismissed their presence as quickly as we had. It might have been arrogant, but if we concerned ourselves with pests like these, we'd never get done.

It was when we were walking back to our car from the first power point of the day that we realized pests could be extremely annoying. Alexa growled as she stared at the slashed tires of her car, garbage bags of collected litter swinging in her hands. "What the heck?"

I walked to the windshield and plucked the note that had been left under the wipers.

This is your final warning. Leave the dragon nests alone or face the consequences!

"Dragon nests?" I asked as I handed the note to Alexa.

"Another term for places of power. Ley line nodes, places of power, dragon nests, same thing," Alexa said as she balled up the paper. She moved to toss it away and then changed her mind almost immediately and stuffed it into her pocket instead.

The initiate quickly popped open the trunk and deposited the collected garbage before she made the call to have her car towed away. "Next time I see them, I'm so going to teach them a lesson."

"Agreed," I said. If those kids thought slashing tires was sufficient a deterrent, they really were imagining things. After all, we were being paid five hundred dollars for every place of power we were sealing. Even if we were stuck taking taxis from location to location, we were still significantly better off.

Later that evening, I was lying in bed, idly listening to the *tap-tap* of keyboard keys as I viewed my character sheet.

Class: Mage
Level 15 (13% Experience)
Known Spells: Light Sphere, Force Spear, Force Shield, Force Fingers, Alter Temperature, Gong, Gust, Heal, Link, Track, Mend, Ward, Glamour, Illusion, Scry, Detect Magic

Magical Skillset
Mana Flow: 3/10
Mana to Energy Conversion: 2/10
Spell Container: 3/10
Spatial Location: 3/10
Spatial Movement: 2/10
Energy Manipulation: 2/10
Biological Manipulation: 1/10

Matter Manipulation: 0/10
Duration: 2/10

As promised, Lily had nerfed my leveling for a bit. I was hoping that I could start leveling at a decent rate soon, but it was not like a video game where everything was run off a series of specific charts. Most of my 'experience' was a rule-of-thumb grant by Lily, much like most of the system. It was intensely frustrating for the munchkin in me that wanted to game the system. However, the constant channeling to the enchanted rods had given me a significant amount of practice, enough so that I had gained a couple of points in Mana Flow and Duration. Even I could tell my body had begun to adjust to the amount of mana I could wield, the headaches in the evening having reduced significantly. Unfortunately, doing the same thing over and over again wasn't helping me develop my spellcasting skills, but that was a different matter.

"Hey, Lily, when am I going to get more matter manipulation spells?" I asked, staring at my greatest weakness.

"When you're ready. You haven't even cast Mend once in the last week," Lily replied immediately. "You got to get your basics right first."

"Oh, come on. I could just get the spell and learn while I cast. Maybe a 'Create Water' or maybe a 'Mud Hole' spell."

"Mud Hole?" Lily asked, a laugh in her voice.

"Or whatever you want to call it. A Bog spell, something to slow people down," I clarified.

"Mmm… maybe." Lily blew a tendril of hair from her mouth. "I still think you need to practice what you know already rather than get more spells."

"But—"

"Did you see the quest list recently?" Lily continued, ignoring my protest.

"No. Figured we'd be doing this for the next few weeks, so I've not been looking," I replied. "Alexa will tell me if there's anything interesting."

"If she was looking," Lily answered. The aforementioned initiate having left to report the damage to her car, it left Lily and I alone in the apartment. "Might be something interesting."

I took the hint and walked over to take a quick look. I paused, sorting through the files for a moment, and looked up, eyebrows drawn downward in concern. "More Devil Rats?"

"Yes."

"Huh." I frowned and pondered the information. After a moment, I pulled out the city map we'd been using and spread it out over the dining room table. I quickly plotted the information on the new rat outbreaks, along with the older rat quests, and stared at the results. "Damn. I think I need to talk to Alexa."

"Talk to me about what?" Alexa asked as she stepped through the doorway.

"Devil Rats."

"That's... interesting," Alexa said after a moment as she stared at the map. Since we only had a single map of the city, we'd previously marked the places of power on it and crossed them out as we went along. Overlaid with the outbreaks of Devil Rats, you could tell that each outbreak was near a place of power. "Not a casual entrance then."

"No. Someone's been opening portals," I said, tapping the map. "What I don't get is why."

"To summon a demon of course," Alexa said.

"Except we never sensed any of that." I pointed to two of the places of power we had sealed, which were near the latest Devil Rat infestations. "And I'm pretty sure I would have. I sensed that imp well before I entered the restaurant, and he was pretty low-powered. I'm sure summoning something more powerful would have left traces."

"True," Alexa said. "Unless they hid it."

"Point." I grimaced. "What do we do now? I'm not exactly thrilled with the idea of trying to take on something more powerful than an imp. Even if we are protected..."

"We do nothing," Alexa said after a moment. She fished her phone out and took a quick photo of the map before furiously texting for a few moments. "Done. I've run this up the chain."

"That easy?" I asked.

"What? You want me to use a courier pigeon?"

"Wasn't what I meant," I said. Though, sending information like this over the Internet, weren't there issues about security? On the other hand, maybe she was using an encrypted app. Were there encrypted apps? "Sorry."

"It's what we do, Henry," Alexa said. "Anyway, with the ring sitting around, we have a few higher-level knights who have need for some serious work in the city."

"Oh." I recalled the people Alexa met with, her continued training in the mornings, and nodded. I guessed this made good use of the resources we had. After all, there was little point in someone following after us, what with the wish blocking most attacks. I took one last glance at the map before I turned away to check on Lily's latest progress in her game, secretly glad it wasn't my problem.

***

"Thank you, sir!" Alexa said, offering a quick peck on the scrapyard owner's cheek before she dropped onto her heels. "We won't be long!"

"No worries, miss. I'm just glad you asked. Not like those other students." The scrapyard owner sniffed and spat to the side. "Always coming in and taking their photos without permission."

"Thank you again!" Alexa waved goodbye and jerked her head toward the inside of the scrapyard. I grunted, following after the blonde. Since Caleb had cancelled our morning appointment, this was our fifth place of power today, and even under my sunglasses, the sunlight was stabbing into my eyes.

"So, what did you tell him?" I asked curiously.

"The truth. We'd been given an assignment by your teacher to check out a few locations in the city," Alexa said.

"And it made that sourpuss let us in?" I asked incredulously, recalling how grumpy the owner had been when we drove up.

"Sometimes, all you have to do is ask. All he wanted was us to acknowledge his rights," Alexa replied sunnily.

In silence, we got down to the task of locating the center of the place of power. The winding pathways in the sprawling location finally brought us to our target, which had me smiling wryly as I stared at the crusher that was smack-dab in the center. Thankfully, it wasn't running this second, but I guessed it made some sense. Countless vehicles and other mementos had bene destroyed by that crusher. All the memories, all the raw emotional baggage, destroyed and focused in that crusher again and again. Even if it was a small amount, years of use would have built up.

I narrowed my eyes, watching the slow swirl of power around the place of power as I judged how much effort would be required. After a time, I slowly nodded to myself and walked forward. From the corner of my eye, I noted Alexa had started to browse the stacks, bored.

Ten minutes later, I wiped my hand across my face, knocking my sunglasses aside slightly. I readjusted them as I looked up to call to my partner. "Hey, I'm done with the first part. Can you… Alexa?"

I frowned, staring around me. After a moment, I shrugged my shoulders and found a comfortable seat out of the sun to rest my eyes, figuring the blonde would find me when she was done. I fished out a pair of painkillers and dry-swallowed the gel pills down, cursing Alexa quietly for taking the water with her. After that, I closed my eyes to rest while I waited for the medicine to kick in.

"Probably shouldn't have pushed for five today," I muttered to myself eventually. The soft crunch of bare earth had me half open my eyes and look up as I began to berate the woman. "You know, for a… what are you—"

"Night, night!" the thin teenager said, a wide grin on his face as he swung the crowbar at my head and interrupted me. I twisted aside too late, the blow landing on top of my head and sending pain exploding through it. Even as I cried out in anguish, a second hit arrived and sent me into peaceful darkness.

Chapter 17

"You need to check on him. This isn't the movies. He could be dying over there!" Alexa's voice came to me as I woke, an unusual thread of concern running through her voice. I groaned as conscious thought returned, along with a splitting pain through my skull and a slight case of wooziness. As I opened my mouth, I felt a slight tug on my scalp, then the cracking of dried blood along with a fresh stab of pain.

"See, he's awake. He's fine," a familiar voice said. "Anyway, you supes are all protected, right? Have some healing factor working for you?"

"That's not true at all! And not if you hit him in the head. Especially not twice. What were you thinking?" Alexa snarled.

"I thought he'd just, you know, fall unconscious," muttered another voice. I recalled this voice, and a flash of anger helped clear some of the woolliness from my brain.

As I shifted, I found I could barely move, my arms, legs, and body tied to a chair. With effort, I cracked my eyes open and regretted the move immediately as ice picks were driven into my head. My eyes watered, and I whimpered as my eyes reflexively shut once more.

"Shit, I think he's got a concussion," Alexa said. "Henry. Don't fall asleep again. Do you hear me? Don't fall asleep. You might die."

"Not true actually," a third, nasally voice said. "Most recent recommendations are for an individual to sleep through minor concussions to increase healing speed."

"What part of cracking his skull is minor?!" Alexa said testily, her voice rising. "If you check my bag, the blue water bottle is a healing potion. If you feed it to him, he'll get better."

"Oooh, let's feed the wizard a potion that we don't know. How dumb do you think we are, lady?"

"Try some of it yourself first then!" Alexa said.

I tried to listen to their conversation further, but the pain in my head pushed against my consciousness, and I faded out. The next thing I knew, someone was dribbling a liquid into my mouth. After spluttering a bit, I eventually swallowed the drink rather than choke to death. You'd think a healing potion would taste good, but mostly it tasted like battery acid. Thankfully, the potion got to work right away as it cleared some of the mushiness in my brain and reduced my pain.

"Man, I should have drunk some of that. Look at the scalp go—"

"Now let us go. If you don't…" Alexa said, her voice rising.

"Oh God, you're going to threaten us now? I think you're misunderstanding the situation you're in," the leader's voice said.

"Please." I groaned. "Please…"

"Go on, Henry," Alexa said encouragingly.

"Shut up!" I said. Each word uttered was a cudgel to my poor senses. Stunned silence filled the room before laughter and giggles exploded from around me.

"You—" Alexa fell silent. However, outside of occasional snorts of laughter, our kidnappers and Alexa thankfully complied with my request.

No longer assaulted by the noise, I focused on the notifications I saw beneath my eyelids.

Henry Tsien dealt 29 damage by Wizard Wannabe.

Henry Tsien dealt 43 damage by Wizard Wannabe.

Henry Tsien has gained 24 health points due to resting.

Henry Tsien has gained 25 health points from Minor Healing Potion.

Once again, I was grateful for the increased healing rate that resting and the system had granted me. Receiving over half my health pool in damage from blows to the head was probably a guaranteed concussion. Heck, the way my thoughts kept shifting and the throbbing pain probably meant I had one, lessened as it was by the potion. However, if we had been kidnapped—and I'd have to assume we had been—lying down on the job was probably not the best option.

I focused, pulling on my mana as I called forth my Heal spell. It was a struggle, the pain and the fact that my arms were tied didn't help. I chanted the words under my breath and failed as an unexpected throb broke my concentration. Again,

I tried and failed. Only on the fourth attempt did I finally get the result I desired.

Heal Cast
24% Synchronicity

Without the system help, I probably couldn't have called the spell into being at all. I groaned slightly as I felt mana quicken the healing process in my body, minor cuts and bruises fixing themselves even as the wound in my head slowly fixed itself.

"Oy! What are you doing," the leader of the teenagers asked and followed it with a kick.

I grunted, my concentration broken and the spell dissipating. The backlash was painful enough that I faded out for a second.

"Gupta. I thought you were watching him."

"Sorry. I was getting a drink," Gupta called. I mentally allocated the voice to the South Asian.

Tired of not being able to see, I started the laborious process of opening my eyes. I cracked them open by a slit, letting them adjust a bit before I stared around the room. I winced, having to pause when my head spun again as I moved too fast once more. Not surprisingly, the idiot teenagers were our kidnappers, the leader of the group glaring straight at me. The room we were in was a dull grey and made of concrete with no external windows, lit by harsh, white fluorescent lamps.

"You doing okay, Henry?" Alexa asked me, her voice low. I turned my head in the direction of her voice, craning my neck to the side to see the initiate trussed up beside me.

"What… what happened?" I slurred slightly, my throat dry.

"I heard something around the corner, and when I went to check it out, they led me on a little chase. By the time I got back, they had you. They threatened to kill you if I didn't give up too," Alexa said.

"You believed them?" I said, staring at the three teenagers who had moved away and were arguing in front of us. From what I could pick up, they were fighting over guard duties. Thinking back to their threat, I couldn't believe it. Sure, they had beaten me up, but kill me? Whatever the movies said, there was a big difference between punching someone and actually killing them. And those three…

"No. But I was scared they'd lose their grip and hurt you. Thought I'd have a chance to turn it around later," Alexa continued to whisper.

"I take it that failed too."

"They're surprisingly good at tying knots," Alexa grumbled and tugged on the arm restraints again to show me. "And they've been keeping a pretty good eye on us. But I'll get us out soon."

"Great. Then I'm going to sleep. Wake me when you're ready," I said.

Alexa opened her mouth to say something else, but the group broke up, and Gupta came back to glare at us. I shut my eyes rather than stare at him, trusting Alexa would come through. In either case, I was of no use to anyone in the condition I was in.

***

"Henry. Wake up. Wake. Up," Alexa half whispered, half hissed at me, pulling me from the comfortable darkness of unconsciousness to the painful reality of life.

Henry Tsien has gained 17 health points due to resting.

Not much of a change, but at least some. I looked over at Alexa when I opened my eyes and then followed her insistent jerking of her head to stare ahead. Gupta had been changed out with Tall-and-Thin, who was sitting on a seat with a graphic novel in his hands, watching us occasionally. The bare concrete floor had been painted on, and a very ornate, mystical-looking magic circle had been drawn on it. It looked all kinds of mystical, but with the knowledge Lily had inserted in my head, it also looked very overdone. Sure, it'd work—the same way a car in the 1900s ran. Wherever the other two were, I couldn't see them with my limited viewpoint.

"This the part they get around to killing us?" I asked Alexa.

"No one's killing anyone," Tall-and-Thin said. "We're not killers."

"Yeah, my concussion says otherwise."

"We healed you," Tall-and-Thin said.

"And we're grateful, Ozzie," Alexa butted in. "Aren't we, Henry?"

I stared at Alexa as she jerked her head toward Ozzie and tried to tell me something with her eyes. After a while, I sighed and nodded in agreement.

"If you aren't about to kill us, what's the plan? Tie us up and make us watch you guys do magic badly?" I asked.

"Oh, no. You're quite important to all this. Well, your blood," the teenage leader said from behind us. He walked around our chairs, interrupting the conversation to smirk at us. I really, really wanted to hit him now.

"Shouldn't you say that with a lisp and some fake fangs?" I asked. "Or are you guys just minions?"

"Neither," the leader growled and kicked my foot.

I winced, and he glared at me.

"It's because of you we're forced to do this. If you'd just listened to our warnings, we could have done this a lot easier."

"Zac, you're about to start monologuing," Ozzie said, dropping a hand on Zac's shoulder.

"Of course I am. That's what bad guys do!" Zac said and grinned.

"Yeah, but—"

"Relax. We've got them tied up. I told you. If they had any real power, they'd have dealt with us already," Zac said, glaring at Ozzie until Ozzie pulled his hand back. Zac turned back to us and smiled. "All we needed was the barrier to drop a little more, and we'd have been able to successfully finish the summoning. But no, you had to kill our Devil Rats. And then, you had to start sealing all the places of power too. So now, here we are."

"You're the idiots summoning the Devil Rats?" I asked. Just as suddenly, pieces started clicking into place. By their very presence, otherworldly beings frayed the edges of our reality. Creatures like the Devil Rats might do only a little, but get enough of them together, and the barriers would drop. These guys didn't have a lot of power, but boosted by a place of power and with a barrier that was lowered, they might actually have been able to summon something. As I looked at Ozzie, the nagging feeling that I'd seen him somewhere before came back along with a memory. The imp.

"Are you insane?" Alexa growled. "Don't tell me you're going to summon a demon to torment the bullies who beat you up?"

"Shut up," Zac said, glaring at the blonde. "I'll let you know nobody bullied me at school." Maybe not Zac, but I noted how both Ozzie and Gupta shifted at Alexa's words.

"If you say you're summoning a devil to trade your souls for power, I'm going to save you the trouble. Those trades never work out the way you think they will." I watched Ozzie and Gupta flinch slightly, and I groaned while Zac just glared at me at first and then his friends.

"We got this. I had my dad help me draft the contract," Zac snapped.

"Your dad?" I cried incredulously. "What is he, a demon lawyer? Wait, are there demon lawyers?" I asked Alexa.

"There are, but—" Alexa paused, shaking her head after a moment. "There's no way it's his dad. We'd know of him if he was."

"My dad's the best corporate lawyer in the state!" Zac snapped even as the pair behind him goggled at the byplay between Alexa and me. "I told him I needed it for my role-playing group, and he helped draw it up."

"You got your dad, a human lawyer, to write up a contract to sign with a demon for your role-playing group." I said the words slowly, hoping Zac could hear how dumb it sounded. Then again, self-delusion was big with this kid. Maybe I needed a bullhorn and some flashing lights too.

"It'll work. And at worse, we'll just send him right back," Zac said.

"You two seem a bit saner. You do understand how messed up this is, right?" I looked past Zac, fixing my gaze on the pair of teenagers behind him. Zac growled and backhanded me, making my headache explode again and stars dance in my eyes. By the time I recovered, I was gagged. When I craned my neck to the side, I noticed Gupta finishing Alexa's gag too.

"That's better. You'll see. You've got a front row seat." Zac reached behind him, pulled out a knife and showed it to me. As I instinctively flinched backward into my chair, Zac sniggered. "Hold him."

Ozzie came forward, gripping my left arm tight before Zac dropped the knife to it and cut my arm free. A brief second later, I felt the blade bite into my flesh followed by the warmth of my blood spilling out. Rather than just leaving a single slice, I felt Zac stab it in again and twist, opening my wound and forcing a muffled scream from my throat. My arm jerked reflexively, and Ozzie had to put his weight on it to keep my arm still as it bled into the iron bucket.

"You didn't have to do that, Zac," Gupta said, his voice filled with worry. "You could really hurt him."

"Fuck him. He's just another damn wizard. The girl will give him another potion to fix him up later anyway," Zac said. "Now he knows not to laugh at me."

I glared at Zac, making a mental note to kick him in the balls a few times when I was out. Alexa next to me had struggled briefly when she'd seen the knife but now had fallen strangely silent. Praying she was working on getting us out of here,

I growled at Zac to keep his attention on me, which just made him smirk.

"That's enough," Ozzie said finally, breaking the silence that had fallen over the group.

Gupta had grown a little pale, having walked away back to their magic circle to study it in detail. Zac continued to smirk at me, watching the blood flow with a little bit too much of a crazy look on his face.

"Just a little more," Zac crooned to Ozzie.

"No. That's enough," Ozzie said and then turned to me, meeting my eyes before he continued. "If you promise not to do anything stupid, I'll get the bandages and wrap you up."

"Mmmphhfff," I mumbled. Taking this as assent, Ozzie moved away and came back, relieved to see I hadn't tried anything. In a few seconds, he had rather expertly bandaged my wound and then tied me to the chair again using the remaining bandages. Obviously, the kid had taken some classes in first aid.

"Good. Now, come on. We can't let the blood get too cold," Zac said as he lugged the pail to the circle. I growled, watching as the group grabbed cups and dipped them into the pail. They took out paintbrushes and went to the circle with my fresh blood.

If it hadn't been my blood, I would have screamed at their laughable incompetence. You didn't need that much blood for a spell or, hell, use the circle itself. You just needed it during the sacrifice. The purpose was the link, which was as much symbolic as it was physical. Sure, more helped, but the amount they'd grabbed from me was ridiculous.

"Stop giggling!" Zac snapped at me as he looked up, and I blinked.

I was not giggling. I was not… right. That was me. I paused, forcing myself to focus again as I realized what had happened. The blood loss really was getting to me. Or was it the concussion? Maybe a little bit of both and the fact that I might actually die here.

Heal.

I needed to heal myself. I focused on that thought, pushing aside everything else, and started my spell. Thankfully, the blood loss seemed less debilitating than the earlier concussion, and the spell kicked off the first time, running through my body and completing the clotting of the wound before it began the process of fixing me.

My kidnappers were too focused on their own task now, Gupta content to stand with his back to me while Zac and Ozzie took station at the other points of the triangle in their freshly painted blood circle. I watched as they began the ritual, chanting together from the pieces of paper they held. After a few seconds, I stopped listening and focused on my spell, unable to grasp the ritual.

It had little to do with the complexities of the ritual or my lack of knowledge, though I'm sure it had something to do with it. But like their ritual circle, much of what they chanted was utter rubbish, made-up words and extra garbage that did nothing but waste time and power. In either case, I had better things to do with my time. Like heal.

I turned my head to the side slowly, careful not to shift too fast or disturb my spell I had cast. Alexa met my eyes when I looked at her, fury radiating from her body as she sat in her chair. A slight movement had me looking down, and that was when I noticed her hand shifting - back and forth ever so gently. My eyes widened, and I looked back at the idiot trio, glad to see they were caught up in their ritual.

Relieved, I focused on our kidnappers and my spell instead, stoking my concentration with the promise of coming revenge. Because what I had seen were the slowly fraying edges of the rope as Alexa cut her way free.

Chapter 18

"*Ilarx Jaa Ba!*" the trio chanted again. This was the third time that had been said, and unlike most of their ritual, those three words made my spine tighten and goosebumps appear on my skin. A part of me knew why—the words were the creature's True Name. It was the most powerful way to call a demon across the barrier and also explained why the trio felt they could do it even with their low level of power. The idiot trio must have had heaven-defying luck to have gotten the True Name of a demon.

Of course, they were also idiots. The True Name of a demon wasn't something you just let others know. It was one of those closely guarded secrets of mages the world over, and the trio had decided to chant it while the initiate and myself were in the same room.

Before I could roll my eyes yet again, the voices of our kidnappers rose in unison, indicating the end of the ritual. I glanced at the notification in the corner of my vision, my lips twisting around the gag.

Henry Tsien has gained 9 health points from Heal.

Not enough time, damn it. I had no choice now as, with the ritual over, the acrid smell of sulfur filled the room and flowed from the circle. Within moments, a demon had appeared. Surprisingly, it stood only five feet tall, its humanoid body covered in light-red scales over paler, pinkish skin beneath. In its mouth, a cigar hung, held in place by a whip-thin tail.

"You called?" the demon said.

"We have summoned you, Ilarx Jaa Ba, to make a deal!" Zac intoned immediately.

"Whoa, you can tone down the theatrics. I'm here already. And you can just call me Il," Il said, waving a hand as he turned to survey the trio. He barely spared any of them a glance before his eyes landed on the pair of us, narrowing.

"We are here… Il… to offer you a deal. A contract," Zac said, his voice losing some of its confidence.

"For your souls, right?" Il interrupted, the horned devil shaking his head. "You three for what, riches and women?"

"What we require is laid out in the document by your feet," Zac replied, gesturing to the bundle of paper.

Il reached out and tapped the document with his foot. For a second, it glowed, and then the entire document burst into flames. "Not interested."

"What? We're offering you—"

"Your souls at the end of your demise. Which will be thousands of years from now at best. Not interested," Il said with a snort. "Anyway, the market for ordinary souls like yours crashed twenty years ago and hasn't recovered. Too many damn collateralized soul obligations that weren't properly insured."

"But—" Zac looked lost, and I snorted through my gag. I glanced at Alexa who sat in her chair stiffly, staring at the demon in our midst.

"Now, for those two…" the demon said and grinned.

"Those two?" Zac asked, turning to stare at us. "I… we…"

"Come now. They are obviously your backup plan. And it's not your soul," Il said, leering at Zac.

"Zac, we can't," Gupta said, glancing down at the burned papers and then us. "This isn't what we agreed to."

Zac stood stock still, not answering his friend. Ozzie stared at Zac, an unreadable expression on his face, while the demon murmured softly, "Women. Wealth. What else do you desire? For those two…"

A tearing of cloth was heard from beside me, so soft I would never have heard it if I hadn't been waiting for that sound for minutes already. I noticed a quick motion, and then suddenly I felt the cold press of iron against my arm. I turned my head to see Alexa sawing at my bindings. Yeah, definitely time to go.

"I can't…" Zac said, his mouth moving and then he straightened his back. "No."

"Fuck that," Ozzie snarled suddenly. "I need that money for my mom. You have a deal, Il."

"Then bring them to me," Il said, grinning as he pointed to us. "Before our prey flees."

My hand free, I raised it and conjured a weak Force Spear. I held it aloft, letting them see the swirling power, an unspoken threat. I saw Ozzie hesitate while Gupta was shouting a denial at Il and Zac was trying to talk sense to Ozzie.

"Free me then, and I'll collect them myself," Il said to Ozzie. "Free me, and our deal is complete. My word on it."

"You can't, Oz," Zac said. Struck by a thought, Zac spun to stare at Il and started speaking some gibberish again.

"Zac. Stop it, don't you dare banish him. Don't! I'm telling you—" Ozzie snarled and then looked at Il, nodding firmly. "Done."

My feet were free, and Alexa was working on the last binding on my left hand. I hadn't dared toss my spear; I didn't know if injuring Ozzie would break the spell even further. However, when I'd heard him speak, I tossed it forward. Unfortunately, my Force Spear had a dozen feet to cross and his foot only had one.

Ozzie's foot rubbed against the circle, smearing dried blood across the ground.

"Thank you," Il said to Ozzie as the demon strolled out of the broken circle, smirking openly and doing nothing to stop my Force Spear. The Force Spear picked Ozzie up and threw him backward, his body flung aside like a ragdoll as my spell collapsed. I had purposely blunted the spear when I'd cast it, not willing to kill just yet.

"Now, let's finish this," Il said as he strolled forward.

I stood quickly, tearing the last of the makeshift bandage restraint off the chair and wincing in pain. Alexa turned and stepped in front of me and to the side, crouching low with her tiny dagger held out in front of her.

"Go, Henry," Alexa snapped after she pulled the gag from her mouth.

"Mmmpff… got this," I said once I managed to extract the gag.

"Really?" Il laughed derisively as he neared us. Behind him, I could see Gupta next to Ozzie, checking him over while Zac stood, frozen in place. When Alexa suddenly stepped forward into a lunge, Il casually moved to block the attack. Both of them suddenly just stood there, staring at each other in shock.

"Told you Lily has this," I said, staring at the information that had just popped up.

Error: Your party member (Alexa) has attempted to engage in an out-of-level encounter.

"What magic is this?" Il snarled. The demon moved swiftly, trying to grab Alexa by the neck, and was once again stopped an inch away from touching her. "You are not this powerful, Wizard!"

"Not me," I said, slowly standing and smiling tightly at the demon. Behind him, I could see Zac's shocked face. "Just a friend. Now, think it's time for you to go home, no?"

Rather than reply to me, I saw Il focus. His light-red skin deepened in color as his hand tightened and the smell of sulfur intensified. Strain as he would, Il progressed no further in his attempts to injure Alexa. In turn, Alexa dropped her hand and focused on Zac and the others. Gupta had finally managed to get Ozzie up and was attempting to skedaddle.

"Fine," Il said finally as he stepped away. "You win this time, Wizard. But I will not be returning empty-handed." As soon as he said that, Il sauntered toward Ozzie and Gupta.

"Henry," Alexa said, her eyes darting between the demon, the trio, and myself. Conflict raged on her face, torn between her duty to safeguard me and her duty to protect others.

"Oh, hell," I said. Pun intended. My mind whirled while I tried to figure out what we could do. I looked again at Il's information.

Ilarx Jaa Ba (Demon Level 40)
HP: ?/?

Not a powerful demon at all. But he was still more than double my level. Even if we somehow blocked him from grabbing the three, Il would just leave and find someone else to drag back. While this was a poor summoning, Il still had more than sufficient strength to do some real damage before he finally lost his corporeal form.

"Stall him," I murmured to Alexa as I hurried to Zac. Il cast a look at me, his lips twisting slightly in amusement, but made no move to stop me. Alexa dashed forward, putting herself between Il and his prey.

"How long would it take to banish him?" I asked Zac, eyeing the pair of pages he still held in his hand.

"Uhh… a few minutes maybe," Zac replied, his voice trembling with fear. "But he has to be in the circle."

I swore silently, knowing Zac was correct. Even broken, the circle still held the power to banish the demon. Outside of it, it would require significantly more strength. Perhaps I could banish him with the ritual myself, but I couldn't be sure. The banishment might only work for those whom had initially participated in the summoning.

At the moment, the demon was glaring at Alexa, who was using her body to block him from moving closer to the pair. Her eyes narrowed as she tried to outguess the demon's intentions. It was a losing proposition though, the demon being faster than my friend.

"Get ready then." I stepped into the circle myself, conjured a Force Bolt, and then cooled the air within it. Once it was sufficiently cold, I lobbed it at Il. Immediately, the Force Bolt dissipated as it hit the unseen barrier around the demon, only the traces of chilled air remaining. Still, it was sufficient to grab the demon's attention.

Error: You are attempting to engage in an out-of-level encounter.

"You attack me?" Il said, eyebrowless brows drawing down as he stared at me, puzzled. In answer, I formed another plain Force Bolt and tossed it at the demon. When he saw the attack dissipate, the demon laughed. "It looks like your protection extends to me as well."

Error: You are attempting to engage in an out-of-level encounter.

"It does," I agreed. as I formed another Force Bolt and tossed it. Il stared at me, obviously curious about what I thought I was doing. He wasn't the only one as Alexa frowned at me.

Error: You are attempting to engage in an out-of-level encounter.
Stop this. If you keep this up, you'll lose your protection.

Finally. I formed another Force Bolt and lobbed it at Il, who had turned around to deal with the two teenagers attempting to sneak away. This Force Bolt glowed as it passed through the barrier before it smashed into the demon's back, throwing him forward from the unexpected force.

Force Bolt does 4 damage to Il.
Out-of-level encounter limitation removed.
You better know what you're doing, Henry.

"Thanks, Lily," I whispered as the information scrolled through.

Il spun around, red eyes glowing with fury, and crossed the room to grab hold of me. His hand closed around my throat and stopped, but this time, it was due to my Force Shield. I just hoped Zac did his job.

"You humans are so predictable. I could tell you were one of those idiotic heroes the moment I saw the pair of you," Il said, his hand beginning to squeeze. I grunted, feeling the Force Shield begin to strain even as Il took his time cracking it. "Did you think you could beat me, Wizard? I can see your strength."

"Fuck. You," I snarled even as my headache intensified. I felt something cut loose, a sharp pain and a light warmth ran down my lips as a nosebleed sprang.

"Pathetic," Il said as he clenched tighter.

My Force Shield shattered, the backlash making me reel. Before his hand could close on my throat, Il screamed as Alexa drove her knife into his back, the knife cutting through his body like butter. Il snarled and slapped Alexa in the face, knocking her down. As he reached down to pluck out the smoking blessed knife that had been left in his body, I raised my hand to cast another spell.

Gong Cast
84% Synchronicity

The spell was focused, channeled around the demon's head. It was so loud that even a few feet away from him, my ears hurt. As for the demon?

Gong does 7 points of damage to Il.
Stunned debuff added.
Deaf debuff added.

Right. That should have made it impossible for the demon to hear Zac at work. Il turned his attention back to me and jabbed a hand outward, reaching for my heart. I stepped back quickly, dodging the grasping hand as I chanted my next spell. A moment later, a Light Ball burst to life in front of Il's eyes, blinding him and me. The moment it did, I let my feet collapse under me, pulling my heels off the ground and letting gravity take over. Not a moment too soon as the blinded demon's hand clawed the air where my chest had been a second ago.

Scrambling on all fours, I moved around the circle that had begun to glow. I jabbed my injured arm down toward the broken spot, my fresh blood reforming the circle with added strength and boosting the banishment spell as I forced my own strength into the circle. I flexed that mystical muscle that controlled my mana flow, pushing more mana into the circle with all my might while attempting to stay in control. My head throbbed further, black spots dancing in my eyes.

As I began to consider what to do next, I felt my foot gripped from behind. Lifted off the ground from my foot, I barely escaped knocking my head on the ground as the five-foot demon proceeded to lift me up with one hand. Luckily for me, the demon was too short for what he wanted to do, so he grabbed hold of my opposite thigh.

"Let go," I snarled as I formed a Force Spear in my hand. I stabbed it into his body as I swung upward. The Force Spear dug into his light, scaled flesh, punching inward a bit. Damage notifications flickered across my eyes, but I ignored them. Il just growled and slapped my hand away. In a second, the Force Spear dispersed.

"You are annoying, Wizard," Il said, eyes narrowed as he glared at me through half-blinded eyes. "I'm going to enjoy hurting you."

The demon punctuated his words by plunging his clawed fingers into my torso, fingers closing on my intestines within. I screamed, the spell I had begun to form again dispersing. Before Il could continue his assault, Alexa, who had crawled over to us, plunged the previously discarded knife into his Achilles tendon and tugged on it, slicing it open.

Unable to support himself, the demon collapsed, his fingers still within my body. I was in so much pain even the addition of the fall and the scrabbling of fingers within my stomach added little to the misery I was in. I couldn't even form a spell the pain was so great.

Henry Tsien dealt 6 damage by falling.
Bleeding debuff received. -4 HP per minute.

Warning: Health is critically low!

"You," the demon snarled, its wound already healing, even around the smoking flesh of the blessed knife. It kicked at Alexa, who managed to get her hand up in time to shield her head. The kick caught her low and picked her up, sending her spinning out of the circle through the air, the dull thump of her landing body making me wince. "You are really getting on my nerves. This ends now."

"Yes, it does," Gupta said as he limped forward and locked hands with Ozzie. Together, the pair made a throwing motion with their hands. A tiny flame floated forward to splash against Il, who stared at them incredulously.

"You used fire? Against me, a demon?" Il said.

"We distracted you," Ozzie said and spit to the side. "Now go to hell."

"What?" Il said and spun around, finally recalling Zac.

The leader of the trio was crouched low, reading the chant. Il snarled and lunged toward Zac, coming to a stop as the circle held him in. He struck it again and again, the once-broken circle beginning to fail again. Head buried in his papers, Zac finally finished the banishment, throwing his hand forward at the end, and a small, black vortex formed in the center of the circle. It pulled Il backward, tearing apart his corporeal body. "No! You humans—"

"Got you." I coughed, clutching my stomach as I watched the demon disappear into thin air. For a second more, I stared at the space where the monster had been before I once again fainted.

Chapter 19

"I have got to stop doing this," I muttered to myself when I woke up again, my last memory of falling unconscious once more. Surprisingly, I didn't hurt, which was an extremely pleasant experience. The fact that I didn't seem to have any recurring side effects from being smacked around so much was amazing. Another surprise was that I wasn't on the concrete floor but my own bed. As I sat up, I spotted Lily tapping away at her laptops but could not find any sign of the initiate.

"She's not here," Lily said to my unasked question. "She's still getting reamed out for nearly getting you killed."

"Speaking of that…" I frowned, touching my stomach as I vividly recalled my lifeblood flowing from it.

"Alexa's people got there before you bled out completely. If Alexa didn't have her training in medicine and her faith-healing ability…" Lily said, trailing off meaningfully as her fingers stopped clicking away. I looked to meet her eyes before I was forced to look aside.

"It was pretty dumb, wasn't it?"

"It was very dumb. But…" Lily paused and then shook her head. The next moment, my status screen appeared in front of my eyes without prompting.

Class: Mage
Level 18 (48% Experience)
Known Spells: Light Sphere, Force Spear, Force Shield, Force Fingers, Alter Temperature, Gong, Gust, Heal,

---

Link, Track, Mend, Ward, Glamour, Illusion, Summon, Iceball, Fireball, Scry, Detect Magic

Magical Skillset
Mana Flow: 4/10
Mana to Energy Conversion: 3/10
Spell Container: 3/10
Spatial Location: 3/10
Spatial Movement: 3/10
Energy Manipulation: 3/10
Biological Manipulation: 2/10
Matter Manipulation: 0/10
Summoning: 0/10
Duration: 4/10

"Wow." I blinked, scanning through the screen for the changes—a couple of levels, a few new spells, more mana flow, control, duration, and biological understanding. "You leveled me."

"You leveled yourself. The numbers are just the reflection of reality. Well, mostly—you pushed yourself and your abilities enough that I could smooth things out a little. Fighting for your life tends to do that," Lily said.

"I guess watching someone do the summoning isn't enough to learn the basics, eh?" I said, and my lip twisted wryly.

"Nor will you yet." Caleb's voice cut into the conversation as he walked into the apartment. I frowned as I watched him put his keys into his pocket as he walked forward. "That is knowledge that you neither require nor are ready to wield."

"Caleb," I said, nodding in greeting to the Mage. "You're back."

"Yes. I leave for a few days, and I find you half-dead upon my return," Caleb said, his voice cold. "Are you attempting to break your own promise? Are you this dead set on ensuring none of us gains the ring?"

"Dead set…" Lily giggled.

"It wasn't like that," I protested, ignoring the jinn. "Though, while you're here, what happened to the idiot trio?"

"The idiot trio, as you called them, have been dealt with. The council has spoken with them, and steps have been taken to ensure they will not be able to repeat their actions. Though, I believe they will not attempt another summoning," Caleb said.

"And Ozzie's mother?" I asked, recalling the boy's impetus.

"Dying from a disease. I forget which one," Caleb answered.

"And you guys are going to help her?" I asked, my eyes narrowing, and Caleb snorted.

"Again, we are not a charitable organization. As it stands, he is lucky we let him live. Summoning a demon, even a low-level one, is a dangerous act."

I growled, shutting my mouth. Still, talking of charitable organizations, I made a note to talk to Alexa about it.

"You know, this entire incident was interesting," Caleb said as he walked toward me, his eyes slightly unfocused as he read my aura. "You risked your life and Alexa's for a group of strangers."

"That's… well…" *What heroes did.* But I couldn't say that out loud. I'd have died of embarrassment.

"Yes, moronic in the extreme. Self-sacrificial. And yet, you gave not a single thought to your friend."

"Alexa? She was about to go ahead and try anyway," I said.

"And still the jinn is not mentioned. One would almost think she was not in danger of being lost for all eternity by your death," Caleb said. I kept my face neutral as he said that, though I found myself shooting a glance at the aforementioned jinn. She continued to focus on her gaming at least.

"Well, she let me," I said finally.

"Still. Interesting, isn't it?" Caleb smiled at me tightly. "I expect you back at class tomorrow." After that last pronouncement, the mage walked out of the room, leaving the pair of us staring at each other in silence.

In the end, I flopped back down onto my bed with a light groan.

***

Alexa returned later that evening, looking worse for wear. The normally energetic blonde looked depressed, her energy shattered by the demands of her bosses. Still, she gave me a smile when she noticed me up and about, puttering around the kitchen making a lasagna.

"Any lasting damage?" Alexa asked as she came to stand beside me.

"None," I told her. "Just one second." I added the lasagna to the preheated oven and set the timer before looking at the initiate. "Thank you. For backing me up."

"Thank you for letting me act," Alexa said. "I know it wasn't an easy choice."

"Actually wasn't that hard," I admitted after a moment. I looked at the blonde, smiling slightly. "I couldn't exactly let a demon run loose. Who would?"

"You'd be surprised," Alexa said with a grimace. I almost asked if her people would have preferred it but restrained myself. Some things were best left alone. "You know, I wondered why God would let such a powerful object fall into untrained, untested hands. Now, perhaps I know why."

"Uhhh… thanks?" I said, looking away. "So… garlic bread?"

Alexa stared at me for a moment before she let the topic go and walked over to the breadbox. "Yeah, I'll get it ready."

I breathed a sigh of relief, watching my partner, my friend, help work on dinner.

Later that evening, I lay on the floor, staring at my ceiling as sleep eluded me. I'd gotten into magic because it was cool, because it had been a lifelong dream to cast spells and be a mage. The reality was every bit as cool as I'd thought it would be, but slinging spells, creating wards, and killing monsters was just the tip of the iceberg. The supernatural world was both more complex than I could ever have imagined and more mundane.

Humans would be humans. Self-interest, greed, and jealousy ruled. We might've had powers beyond the normal, but everyone was still intent on doing what was best for themselves and their groups. Well. Most everyone.

I'd done quests because it was the best way to make money and level up. But I never really thought about why I'd bothered, why I'd done it. Hell, I'd even started acting like Caleb, laughing and deriding the idiot trio because they couldn't really wield magic like I did. But, in the end, for all their own desires, they'd stepped up and helped thrust the demon back into hell.

That was the thing, power for the sake of power was vanity. The best times I'd had were when my quests actually had a purpose, when I was helping others.

Maybe, just maybe, it was time for me to start thinking less like a gamer and more like a person.

###
THE END

Thank you for reading *A Gamer's Wish*! Henry's adventure continues in *A Squire's Wish*.

Let's stay connected!
Be the first to hear about new books, special offers, and exclusive content:

Author's Note

Thank you for reading my attempt at an urban fantasy, GameLit world. It was an interesting experience writing this novel, mixing gaming along with some urban fantasy tropes. I'm not entirely sure it worked well, but I enjoyed visiting with Lily and Henry.

A Squire's Wish (book 2 of the Hidden Wishes series) has now released and is available for purchase at:
-    https://books2read.com/squires-wish

As always, if you enjoyed reading the book, please do leave a review and rating.

Please check out my other series, the Adventures on Brad (a slice-of-life fantasy LitRPG), the System Apocalypse (a post-apocalyptic LitRPG) and A Thousand Li (a cultivation xanxia series). Book one of each series is named:
-    A Healer's Gift (Book 1 of the Adventures on Brad)
     https://books2read.com/healers-gift
-    Life in the North (An Apocalyptic LitRPG)
     www.starlitpublishing.com/collections/the-system-apocalypse
-    A Thousand Li (a cultivation series inspired by Chinese wuxia and xianxia novels)
www.starlitpublishing.com/collections/a-thousand-li

In addition, please take a look at other series/books I have co-written:

- **Leveled up Love!** by Tao Wong & A. G. Marshall
  https://books2read.com/leveled-up-love
- **A Fist Full of Credits** by Tao Wong & Craig Hamilton (Book 1 of System Apocalypse: Relentless)
  www.starlitpublishing.com/collections/system-apocalypse-relentless
- **Town Under** by Tao Wong & K.T. Hanna (Book 1 of System Apocalypse: Australia)
  www.starlitpublishing.com/collections/system-apocalypse-australia

For more great information about LitRPG series, check out the Facebook groups:
- Gamelit Society
https://www.facebook.com/groups/LitRPGsociety/
- LitRPG Books
https://www.facebook.com/groups/LitRPG.books/

If you'd like to support me directly, I now have a Patreon page where previews of all my new books can be found!

- https://www.patreon.com/taowong

About the Author

Tao Wong is the author of the A Thousand Li progression fantasy series and the System Apocalypse LitRPG series, among others. His work has been released in audio, paperback, hardcover, and ebook formats, and translated into German, Spanish, Portuguese, Russian, and several other languages.

He was shortlisted for the UK Kindle Storyteller Award in 2021 for A Thousand Li: The Second Sect. In 2026, the first three books in the A Thousand Li series will be republished in hardcover by Ace Books. When he's not writing or working, he enjoys practicing martial arts, reading, and dreaming up new worlds. He lives in Toronto, Canada.

For updates on the series and his other books (and special one-shot stories), please visit the author's website: http://www.mylifemytao.com

Subscribers to Tao's mailing list will receive exclusive access to short stories in the Thousand Li and System Apocalypse universes: https://www.subscribepage.com/taowong

Or visit Tao's Facebook Page: https://www.facebook.com/taowongauthor/

About the Publisher

Starlit Publishing is an indie publisher producing works in the science fiction and fantasy genres with a specific focus in the LitRPG and xianxia fantasy genres.

As a publisher, Starlit Publishing releases five to ten books in the English language a year, with a backlist of over forty books, multiple novellas and short stories. Books published are created and licensed for distribution as ebooks, paperbacks, hardcovers and audiobooks as well as serials across the world, with translations in multiple languages.

Starlit Publishing is owned by Tao Wong and based in Toronto, Ontario, Canada.
For more information on Starlit Publishing, visit their website:
https://www.starlitpublishing.com/

You can also join Starlit Publishing's mailing list to learn of new, exciting authors and book releases.
https://starlitpublishing.com/newsletter-signup/

A Squire's Wish (Book 2)
Sample Chapter

"This would be a lot easier if I was allowed to use magic." I exhaled audibly and twisted my shoulders, my arms throbbing. Still, at least we were finally inside our new duplex. Three bedrooms, two bathrooms, hardwood floors, and a living room meant I was paying much more than I wanted. But, considering Alexa had insisted on the larger space, and she was paying half, I'd compromised. I had to admit, looking around the relatively modern, open-plan space, it looked nice. Even if all the belongings I had from my bachelor suite barely filled our new home.

"Oh please, this is barely a workout," Alexa said as she impatiently tapped her foot. The Nordic blonde was more Wonder Woman than model and had more muscles in her arms than I did, so it was no surprise she was barely out of breath.

"Mage," I said and pointed to myself as I struggled to catch my breath. Though perhaps I could do with a little more actual exercise.

"The enforcers in the Mage Council are as well known for their physical prowess as they are for their magical abilities," Alexa said. I grunted, refusing to acknowledge her point, even while being intrigued by the idea of buff magic users. I guessed real-world magicians were more like anime heroes than Raistlin. In either case, the initiate was more likely to know than I did. The Templars had been the church's sharp edge against the supernatural world for hundreds of years. They'd been occasional allies and enemies of the Mage Council throughout the years. Me? I'd barely entered the supernatural world six months ago. I still had a lot to catch up on.

"Fine. So I might be slacking off on the entire exercise bit," I muttered as I bent my knees to grab the edge of the couch once again.

"Slacking off implies you ever started," Lily said behind me, her arms full with a cardboard box helpfully labeled "books." The olive-skinned, slim and shapely jinn sauntered toward us from the front door where we'd deposited our initial run with a sway of her hips. "Where do you want these?"

"What are they?" I grunted out as we maneuvered the couch to catch the sunlight and to face where we'd decided the TV would go.

"Reference material."

"Huh?" I said as I squatted and set my end of the couch on the floor.

"Your role-playing books." The jinn held the heavy box of books with one hand as she scratched her nose, obviously not bothered with things like weight. No surprise there. Her "body" wasn't really real, just a magical construct, which begged the question why I was doing the heavy lifting, but that would open up a whole different can of worms regarding Lily's increasing agoraphobia.

"Right. We'll keep those in the living room," I said and pointed to the corner we'd designated for the bookcases. For a moment, I felt amazed as the reality of my situation hit me once again. Not the shacking up with two stunning, supermodel-level, good-looking women but the fact that I was a mage—a mage wielding magic through a wish granted by a jinn who based my entire leveling progression off a homebrew mixture of role-playing game books, single-player video games, and massive multiplayer online games. It was how my old RPG books became reference material.

"Stop delaying. We've only got the moving van till five," Alexa said, urging me out the front door.

"You sure I can't do this with magic?"

"After you left the dent in the doorway of our old apartment?" Alexa said derisively. "We can't afford to pay to fix another mistake."

"Fine." I grumbled as we reached the moving van and went for the bed stand. Alexa was not wrong. We still needed to find the money for mattresses and bed frames for both girls. Or technically, for me since I'd given my bed to Alexa. "Let's get this over with."

***

Hours later, the three of us were seated in our new living room, evening sunlight streaming in from the blinds as we preyed on four large pizzas. I shook my head, amazed once again at the sheer volume of food both women managed to put away. Admittedly, today I was putting on a good showing. Not that it was a competition.

"So, Caleb gave you today off? Alexa asked.

"Yes. After I threatened to continue using 'What Does the Fox Say?' as my training tune for Gong," I said with a grin. Since Lily basically downloaded spells into my brain at each level increase, my understanding of actual magical theory was, shall we say, erratic. It didn't help that much of the magic theory she downloaded came from millennia of magical knowledge—knowledge gained as the assistant or tool of world-class magicians. While I might have more powerful spells than my more traditionally trained counterparts, mine were also more esoteric and not as easily pliable with modern magical theory. To fix my magical shortcomings, Caleb, the master mage sent to deal with me from the Mage Council, had set up a training program. One aspect of which was teaching me to understand and manipulate the components of the spells I had in my brain.

In the case of Gong, the spell manipulated sound waves via magic. Like most spells, Gong, for all its outward simplicity, was significantly more complex internally than its final manifestation. To channel the spell, I had to control the amount of mana input, where the mana went to adjust volume and pitch, as well as dictate the location the noise would appear. All this was controlled by strings of arcane glyphs and, in some cases, actual mathematical formulas. Combined, they were

296

known as spell formulas. Right now, my training involved learning to repeatedly cast the spell with specific target notes. I had to play a song with my spell.

Technically, I was doing this in the least mana efficient manner possible. There were actual spells that allowed its user to continually channel the spell, formulating the song in one continual cast. The problem was the spell formula for such a song was significantly more complex than the simple spell Lily had downloaded into my mind. It was kind of like the difference between playing "Chopsticks" and Mozart. When I'd asked, Caleb had displayed the simplest musical spell formula he knew for me to read just to shut me up. The formula itself was intriguing, a mixture of—

"Earth to Henry," Lily said, waving a hand in front of my eyes.

"Sorry," I said, pushing her hand away. "Was just thinking of a spell."

"Of course you were," Lily said with a snort. "Maybe you should be thinking about a quest instead. If you haven't forgotten, you're broke."

"We're broke," I said pointedly. "I still don't get why you need a room of your own. You have your ring."

"Which I've lived in for hundreds of years," Lily said, glaring at me. "You try going back to your cell. Even if the door's open—"

"Ah, right," I said and scratched my head. Sometimes I forgot Lily was basically a slave to the ring since she never actually lived in it anymore. While she had twisted my first wish to give her a way to stay out of the ring itself, past users hadn't been as careless or generous. "Sorry."

"It's fine," Lily said with a wave of her hand.

"I do not understand, however, why you cannot form your own furnishings," Alexa asked Lily.

"If you recall, I'm bound by the rules of the ring. I can't really affect the outside world in a meaningful manner with my magic without a wish," Lily said with a little bite. I guess some insults, like the Templars trying to kill me and steal my ring via Alexa, were not so easily forgiven.

"Wait. With your magic?" I said. "I thought you couldn't do it period."

"Well…" Lily paused, looking embarrassed. "It's a bit complicated."

"Complicated… like you-don't-want-to-get-a-job complicated?" I said threateningly. While I'd been scrambling to earn an income by completing requests and other small jobs in the magical community, Lily had stayed home playing computer games… and begging me to get a console.

"Well, I'm not exactly legal, am I?" Lily asked. "I don't have any proof of identification. You wouldn't want me to be deported or thrown into jail, would you?"

"That…" I paused to consider as I looked at Lily. Well, yes. She was a Middle Eastern woman in the country. Technically illegally. Then again, she was a jinn who could literally disappear with a thought, which would make for a really interesting police report. But… "Thousand hells."

"Right," Lily said with a smile when she won her point. "That's why it's better I stay back home. Also, the more games I play, the better the patches I can provide."

Once again, I noted how she also avoided mentioning her growing reluctance to even visit the outside world. I considered bringing it up and once again shied away from the topic. Tackling sensitive emotional issues headlong was not something my traditional Chinese household had readied me for.

"Please don't." Alexa interrupted my thoughts with her words. "Your last patch had him sitting at the beach picking up rocks for an hour, muttering about leveling up his 'analyze' skill."

"Hey, it's a staple cheat skill," Lily said.

"Not the way you implemented it," I said. It was only after I had spent some time talking to Lily that I realized the only way to upgrade the analyze skill while staring at rocks would have been to read books on geology first, then spend the time actually perusing the rocks. And then repeating the task over and over again.

"Everyone's a critic," Lily said and crossed her arms to glare at us.

"As the lab rat, yes I am," I said. "Let's just focus on magic, okay?"

"Speaking of that, what are your… stats?" Alexa said, almost too casually. Really, the knight initiate sucked at casual. It just wasn't something they taught at knight school. It didn't help that I knew she was asking because the Templars, like most of the other major powers in the know, were waiting for me to hit level one hundred. Once I did, the ring could finally come off my fingers without it being lost forever.

Still, she was my closest ally. And I had no reason not to show her since Caleb received almost daily updates.

Class: Mage
Level 21 (19% Experience)
  Known Spells: Light Sphere, Force Spear, Force Shield, Force Fingers, Alter Temperature, Gong, Gust, Heal, Healing Ward, Link, Track, Fix, Ward, Glamour, Illusion, Summon, Iceball, Fireball

Magical Skillset
Mana Flow: 4/10
Mana to Energy Conversion: 3/10
Spell Container: 3/10
Spatial Location: 3/10
Spatial Movement: 3/10
Energy Manipulation: 4/10
Biological Manipulation: 3/10
Matter Manipulation: 1/10
Summoning: 1/10
Duration: 4/10

"You gained two levels," Alexa said in approval. "But only learned one new spell?"

"Blame Caleb," I said, disgruntled. "He convinced Lily I needed to spend more time understanding my current repertoire. He wants her to stop giving me spells entirely."

"That," Alexa said and then fell silent, compressing her lips together tightly on the sentence she had been about to utter.

"Sucks. I know." I sighed. Truth be told, I somewhat agreed with Caleb's reasoning. I'd gained so many spells, I often did not use most of them. For quite a few, I had synchronicity of less than 50 percent when I cast them, never mind linking them together. No, for a while, I needed to work on my fundamentals. If I could increase my basic magical skill set to five, I'd be considered an actual novice mage by the Council, someone who at least was worth some basic respect. Of course, the fact this was a logarithmic progression meant that once I got there, the next steps were going to be incrementally harder.

"So. Quests," Lily said leadingly, pushing forth a sheaf of papers. I groaned, staring at the quests— work orders, really—but picked them up. We needed the money.

Read more:

https://books2read.com/squires-wish